# THE WHOLE WORLD STORYBOOK

# The Whole World Storybook

Marcus Crouch

*Illustrated by William Stobbs*

Oxford University Press

OXFORD TORONTO MELBOURNE

Oxford University Press, Walton Street, Oxford OX2 6DP
*London Glasgow New York Toronto*
*Delhi Bombay Calcutta Madras Karachi*
*Nairobi Dar es Salaam Cape Town Salisbury*
*Kuala Lumpur Singapore Hong Kong Tokyo*
*Melbourne Auckland*

and associates in
*Beirut Berlin Ibadan Mexico City Nicosia*



*British Library Cataloguing in Publication Data*
The whole world storybook.
1. Children's stories, English
I. Crouch, Marcus
823'.01'089282[J] PZ5
ISBN 0–19–278103–0

Typeset by Western Printing Services Ltd, Bristol
Printed by Butler & Tanner Ltd., Frome

# CONTENTS

*This book is for*
*Samantha*
*and*
*Bill's Half-Dozen*

GREECE

# LAZARUS AND THE DRAGONS

LAZARUS the cobbler was in a paddy. Every time he settled down to work, a swarm of flies buzzed around his head and put him off his stitch. At last he grabbed a strip of leather and lashed about him. When he stopped, what do you think? Forty flies lay crushed and dead.

What a warrior! He stood for a moment in silence, overcome at the thought of his valour. Then he carved himself a wooden sword and wrote on the blade: WITH ONE BLOW I SLEW FORTY. Then he locked up his shop and set out, looking for adventure.

He had been on the road a couple of days when he came to a spring and, liking the look of the place, he lay down there and slept. Now, not far off lived a colony of dragons and this was their water-supply. In the morning one of the dragons came to fetch water, and there lay Lazarus. The dragon spelt out the words on the sword, and he ran back and told his companions.

'Forty at a blow, hey!' they said. 'It will pay us to keep on the right side of that one. Go and ask him to join our company.'

That is what the messenger dragon did, and you may be sure that it took Lazarus no time at all to decide to accept. So up he got and made camp in the dragon's cave.

Now the dragons used to take it in turn to go for water and firewood. Soon it came to Lazarus's turn to fetch the water. They gave him a water-skin which held two hundred gallons. It was as much as Lazarus could do to drag this empty to the spring; he knew very well that he would never shift it when it was full. Instead, he began to dig a trench round the spring, sweating in the hot sun as he worked.

The dragons thought he was taking a long time, so they sent to see what had gone wrong. The messenger dragon said: 'What are you up to, Lazarus?'

'Oh, I can't be bothered to keep going to the spring for water. I thought I'd just bring the whole spring up to the cave.'

'Don't do that, for goodness sake,' said the dragon. 'When that is gone we shall all die of thirst. Leave it. We will do your share of water-carrying.'

That suited Lazarus well.

Soon it was Lazarus's turn to go for wood for the fire. What the dragons used to do was just pull up a single tree by the roots and drag it back to the cave. Of course Lazarus was not strong enough to shift a single branch. So he set to, looping a long cord round all the trees in the wood. This took a long time, and the messenger came to see what was keeping him.

'What are you doing now?' said the messenger.

'Oh, I thought I'd bring the whole wood along to save time.'

'Let it alone,' said the dragon. 'If you destroy the whole wood we shall starve of cold in the winter. Forget it, and we'll do your wood-gathering for you.'

This was all very well for Lazarus, but the dragons grew impatient, seeing him lying around idly every day. They decided to make away with him. One had one idea, one another, but in the end they agreed to kill him with an axe during the night. But Lazarus overheard their plotting. That night he put a log into his bed and wrapped it up in his cloak. In the dark the dragons came crowding in, each with his axe. They all hacked away at the bed and then went away, chuckling at their cleverness.

Lazarus threw away the battered log and lay down on the bed. As morning came, he began to mutter to himself. The dragons heard him and came, very much surprised, to his bedside. 'What are you saying?' they asked.

'Those fleas!' he said. 'They have given me no peace, biting and nibbling at me all night long.'

The dragons held another meeting. 'What's the

use?' they said. 'If he thinks our axes are just flea-bites we shall never get rid of him by force.' So they went to him and said: 'Don't you think it is time you went home to your wife and family? You must surely be missing them. We will give you a sack of gold if you go quietly and give no more trouble.'

'I have never given any trouble,' said Lazarus. 'But if you are tired of me, you have only to say so. I don't want to be a burden. But one of you can come along and carry the sack.'

When they were nearly home, Lazarus said: 'Just wait here. I must go ahead and tie up my children. If I don't, they will surely eat you up.'

Home ran the cobbler, and weren't his children glad to see him? But he told them to stand still while

he tied them up with rope. 'Now,' he said. 'When I come back with the dragon, be sure to shout out "Dragon Meat!" as loud as ever you can.'

That is what happened. As soon as the dragon came in sight, all the children shouted 'Dragon Meat!', and the poor dragon dropped the sack and ran for his life.

He had gone a mile or two, and was quite out of breath, when he came up with a fox. 'What's the panic?' he asked, and the dragon gasped out his story.

'Surely you are not afraid of Lazarus's kids!' said the fox scornfully. 'Why, the man owns nothing but a brace of hens, and I ate one of those yesterday, and here is the other ready for my supper tonight. He is nothing to be scared of, or his family either.'

'He's a terrible man,' moaned the dragon.

'Nonsense! Come with me and see for yourself. If you are so afraid, tie yourself to my tail and I'll protect you.'

So back they went to the cobbler's house, tied by their tails.

Lazarus had guessed that he might not have seen the last of his dragon friend, so he was on the look-out, armed with a gun.

He saw the two animals approaching, and he shouted to the fox: 'Hey there, Bushytail! I thought I told you to collect all the dragons, not just one.'

With a squeal of fright the dragon turned and ran, dragging the fox with him for a couple of miles until the fox's fine tail came out by the roots and he was left bleeding by the wayside.

As for Lazarus, he and his children went without dragon-meat for supper, but they had plenty of gold to live on for the rest of their days.

RUSSIA

## HALF-RAM LEAVES HOME

THERE was a rich farmer who wanted a new coat for the winter. So he had five of his sheep killed and skinned, and he sent the hides to the tailor to be made up into a coat.

The tailor set to work, but he soon found that he had not enough material to finish the job. He was short of just half a skin.

'That's no problem,' said the farmer when he was told. 'Here, John. Catch that fat ram and strip off half his skin!' And that is what they did.

The ram had worked faithfully for his master for many years, and he was very angry at being treated like this. Bleeding and sore, he went to find his friend the goat. 'I'm not stopping here another day,' he said. 'There is a good living to be had in the woods, and no one there will rob you of your skin just to keep his own selfish hide warm.'

The goat agreed, and the two animals went off to the forest where they built themselves a little hut against the weather, and there they lived very well. News of what they had done got back to the farm, and several other animals decided to follow their example. First a cow, then a pig, a cock and a gander left home. They wandered on together until they came to the hut.

'Let us come in,' they said. 'It's getting chilly and winter is on the way.' The ram and the goat refused and drove the other animals away. After a while the cow came back to the hut alone. 'Let me in,' she said, 'or I'll lean on the walls and your hut will fall down.'

The ram thought it prudent to oblige her, and she squeezed through the door. Next came the pig. 'Let me in, or I'll dig under the walls and let the cold air in.' 'Come in, Pig, and welcome', said the ram. That made four in the little hut. Very soon the gander was tapping on the door. 'Let me in, or I'll peck a hole in the wall and the wind will get in.' In he came, and in a minute or two the cock was at the door. 'Let me in, or I'll tear the thatch off the roof.' So there they were, six good friends living together in one little hut.

One night a band of robbers came that way, and they were surprised to hear strange noises coming from the hut. They could not guess what it might be, so they told one of the gang (who was the smallest and the most easily frightened) to go in and find out if the hut was worth robbing. 'Or else,' they said, 'we'll throw you in the river!'

The small robber was not keen to go, but he had no choice. He pushed open the door and stepped into pitch darkness. There was a dreadful noise, and out he came backwards with great force. He and his companions did not stop running for half a mile.

'What happened?' they asked, when at last they paused for breath.

'Well, brothers,' he gasped. 'You may drown me, or burn me, but you won't get me inside that hut again. Directly I put my nose in a woman began to hit me with an oven fork. Then her daughter joined in. Next a cobbler stuck his awl into my back. Then a tailor started on me with his scissors. Next it was the turn of a soldier who jumped on my back and dug spurs into me, while he yelled his horrible war-cry. I won't go there again, that's for sure.'

'We shan't get much profit there,' said the others, and so they moved right out of that part of the forest.

After that the animals were left undisturbed for many a day. They lived together contentedly, but not all the neighbours cared for their company. They were often noisy, and smaller creatures found that their prey had been frightened away. So the animals made themselves enemies among the rats and hedgehogs of the woods.

One night a pack of wolves came hunting. At once they recognized the farm animals by their smell. Here was a good dinner waiting to be picked up. One of the pack leapt into the hut, but all the animals set on him together and gave him a sound thrashing, so that he was lucky to get away with his life.

The wolves drew back to a safe position and sat down to discuss what was to be done. They argued and argued, but could not agree on a plan. Then a small voice came from the ground: 'I can help you.' It was one of the hedgehogs who lived nearby and who had no cause to love the farm animals. He whispered his plan, and the wolves saw that it was good. One wolf went ahead and pushed open the door of the hut. The hedgehog ran inside and stuck his prickles into the raw flank of the ram. The ram gave one loud bleat and ran, and all his friends ran with him. Then the wolves moved into the hut and made it their own home.

FINLAND

# OLLI THE TERRIBLE

THERE was this farmer. An honest enough fellow he was and hard-working, but he never seemed to have two coins to rub together. It used to make him mad to see how his neighbour, who was a wicked troll, had amassed a huge fortune of gold and jewels.

One day the farmer said to his three sons: 'You know, it's time someone did something about that troll. Here we are, working ourselves to the bone, while he sits back and rolls in wealth. If you had anything at all about you, you would go and help yourselves to a few handfuls of his gold.'

'I'll go,' said the youngest boy, whose name was Olli.

'Listen to baby brother!' scoffed the others. 'He is always pushing himself forward.' And to their father they said: 'Right ho. We will go along and give that old troll a good shake-up. Olli can come and watch, if he wants.'

So next morning off went the three brothers. They walked along the shore and up the mountain until they came to the troll's house. The troll and his wife greeted them warmly.

'It is good to see you, neighbours,' said the troll. 'I've been watching you lads growing up over the years, and fine young men you have become. Now I have three pretty young daughters of my own. Why shouldn't we make a match of it? Become my sons-in-law and you can have all my wealth when I am gone.'

'Don't listen to him,' whispered Olli, but the elder brothers were delighted and shook hands on the bargain.

The troll's wife cooked a big meal for them, and when they had eaten their fill the three brothers went up to bed with their new wives. As they were going upstairs the troll handed each brother a red nightcap, and he put a white one on each of the girls.

The elder brothers were soon asleep, but Olli lay wakeful, thinking. After a while he slipped out of bed, took the three red caps, and exchanged them for the girls' white caps. Then he lay down and waited to see what might happen.

Very soon he heard the troll come into the room. The giant had a knife in his hand. Peering into the darkness, he could just distinguish the red and white caps. With three quick slashes he cut off the heads beneath the red caps. Then he went back to bed, and Olli heard him chuckling with his wife.

Olli shook his brothers awake, and they crept quietly out of the house and hurried home.

The brothers were thankful to have got back with their heads still firm on their shoulders, and they showed no wish to return. Olli used to tease them, saying: 'Come on, let's call on the troll.' They always shook with fear and told him not to be such a fool.

One day Olli said: 'I am told the troll has a horse with a mane of gold and silver. I think I'll go and take it off him.'

The others did their best to persuade him not to go, but he just wouldn't listen. He went off very cheerfully, shouting: 'I am walking away but I'll ride home.'

This time the troll was out, but his wife was at home and she let Olli in. She recognized him at once, and thought of a way to keep him busy until the troll got home. 'I am so pushed today,' she said. 'Will you be a good boy and take the horse down to the lake and water him?'

'To be sure,' said Olli, but directly he was on the horse's back he galloped away and rode straight home.

Late that night the troll came down to the shore and shouted across to Olli's farm: 'Olli, are you there?'

'Here I am,' shouted Olli.

'Have you got my horse?'

'Well, I had your horse, but it's my horse now.'

Olli was pleased with his day's work, but his father was frightened of the troll's anger, and the brothers were jealous of Olli's fine gold and silver horse.

During the next few days Olli was happy enough, riding his new steed, but then he grew restless.

'I think I'll go over and steal the troll's money-bag today,' he said.

Father was horrified, but the boy would not be guided by him. He strode off and found the troll's wife alone again.

She saw him coming and said to herself: 'Oh dear! Here's that terrible Olli. I mustn't let him get away until my husband comes home to deal with him.' So she pretended to make him welcome, and gave him something to eat while she went on with her housework.

After a while she began to yawn and rub her back. 'I must just lie down for a while,' she said. 'Be a good boy and watch the oven for me, and don't let the bread burn.'

He did this, and the old woman lay down but kept half an eye on him. But she really was tired, and very soon she had dropped off to sleep.

'This is it,' said Olli to himself. He knelt down beside the bed and pulled out the troll's money-bag from under it. He slung it over his shoulder and hurried home.

That night the troll came to the shore and shouted across to Olli's farm: 'Olli, are you there?'

'Here I am.'

'Have you got my money-bag?'

'Well, I had your money-bag, but it's my money-bag now.'

Olli was still not satisfied. In a day or two he said to his father: 'I noticed that troll had a fine cover on his bed. It was woven in silk and gold thread. I think I'll have it.'

Again his father was terrified, but Olli would not listen. He waited until it was getting dark, then he took a can of water and a drill, and he went quietly to the home of the sleeping troll. He clambered on to the roof and bored a hole in it with his drill. The bed was just underneath. He took his can and let water dribble from it on to the bed. The troll woke up.

'I'm wet,' he shouted. 'I'm soaked, and so is the bed.'

His wife struggled out of bed. 'The roof must be leaking,' she said. 'I told you to get it fixed after that last gale.'

She pulled the cover off the bed and slung it across the rafters to dry. Then they settled down again and were soon asleep.

Olli enlarged the hole he had made until he could get his hand in. Then he pulled the bed-cover out. Home he went, well pleased with his night's work.

In the morning the troll shouted across to Olli's farm: 'Olli, are you there?'

'Here I am.'

'Have you got my bed-cover?'

'Well, I had your bed-cover, but it's my bed-cover now.'

Later that same week Olli said to his father:

'There is just one more thing I want out of that old troll. He has a golden bell which would look just right in our house.'

So off he went that night, carrying his drill and a saw. He waited until he could hear the trolls snoring, and then he cut a hole in the side of the house. He put his hand in very carefully to get the bell. But when he touched it, it gave a loud 'Ting!' The troll awoke at once and grabbed Olli's hand. 'Now I've got you,' he said, and he dragged the boy into the house.

'I think we'll eat him,' said the troll. 'Make a good fire, wife, and we will roast him.'

The troll's wife got a roaring fire going in the oven. The troll was delighted. He kept pinching Olli's arms and legs and saying: 'He will make a fine dinner.' Then he thought for a moment and said: 'He's too good to waste. I will invite the neighbours and we can have a real feast. I'll go and get them. You keep the fire up and, when the oven is ready, just push him in and he'll be done to a turn by the time I get back.'

'Don't be long,' she said. 'He's very tender, and we don't want him overdone.'

The troll went off, chuckling at the thought of the treat to come. His wife watched the fire until the oven was just right. Then she raked out the cinders and said to Olli: 'Now, my lad! Just sit with your back to the oven and your knees up and I'll push you in.'

Olli sat down, first one way, then another way, but no way would he fit into that oven. She got so impatient. 'Hunch yourself up and tuck your elbows in,' she shouted.

'I'm sorry,' said Olli. 'I just don't seem to get it

right. Could you show me how?'

So the old woman sat with her back to the oven and screwed herself into a ball.

'Oh, I see,' said Olli. 'Then you push me in and slam the door, like that!' And he gave her a good shove and into the oven she went, and he shut the door firmly after her.

Olli left her there, and when she was well done he took her out and got her ready for the table. Then he found a sack, stuffed it with straw, and dressed it in some of the troll-wife's clothes. He lay this on the bed, and it looked just like the old woman asleep. After that he picked up the golden bell and went home.

Soon—what a noise!—the troll came back, bringing all his troll friends and neighbours.

'That smells good!' they all shouted.

'Ah! The old woman's asleep,' said the troll. 'It would be a shame to wake her. Besides, there'll be all the more for us.'

So they sat down, and a very good meal they made.

After a while the troll's knife hit something hard. 'That's funny,' he said. 'Here is one of my old woman's beads. How did that get there?'

He got up and walked over to the bed to ask his wife. When he came back to the table he had turned green and was shaking his head. 'I'm sorry, lads,' he said. 'We've made a bad mistake. We've eaten the old woman, not the boy. It's too bad! Still, we may as well finish her now.'

So they went on feasting till night gave way to dawn.

Then the troll went and shouted across to Olli's farm: 'Olli, are you there?'

'Here I am.'

'Have you got my golden bell?'

'Well, I had your golden bell, but it's my bell now.'

'Another thing, Olli. Did you roast my old woman?'

'Your old woman? Why, isn't that her right behind you?' And Olli pointed behind the troll at the rising sun.

The troll looked round. Now trolls can't look at the sun or they burst. And that is just what this troll did!

So that was that. Olli never had any more trouble with trolls. The word got around, and no troll, however big or wealthy, was prepared to tangle with Terrible Olli.

ZAÏRE

## A PAIR OF SKINNIES

THERE never was such a skinny old man, and his wife was no fatter. They lived all alone in a hut on the edge of the forest. The villagers mostly left them to themselves, because whenever you visited them they did nothing but moan about how ill they were and how poor and hungry. Besides, if you did call on them you usually found, when you got back home, that you had lost something; money or a bit of an ornament or even a scrap of food.

As time went on the skinny old couple were left more and more to their own affairs until, just for company, they took to walking in to the village. One day a man who had kept to his hut because he was feeling unwell woke up just in time to see the skinny couple sneaking out through his door. He shouted at them and they ran off like two scared rabbits. He went on shouting until the neighbours came to see who was being killed.

'It's that skinny couple,' said the sick man. 'They came creeping in here while I was asleep, and now they have gone off with all my money.'

'Don't you worry,' said the neighbours. 'We'll deal with those two.' Then they went off in a crowd to the home of the skinny couple. The two were lying in bed, looking as if they had never done anything wrong in all their lives.

'Where's the bag of money?' shouted the neighbours. 'Give it back or we will whip you until you bleed.'

The old folk wept and cried and said they had taken no money, and, sure enough, when the neighbours searched the hut they could find no sign of it. They were not satisfied, though, because they did not trust that pair one bit. 'We'll be back,' they said, 'and then you will have a good taste of whip.'

Directly they were out of sight, the skinny couple jumped out of bed and rummaged in the thatch of the roof and pulled down the bag of money which they had hidden there. Then they scuttled away into the forest. The returning villagers saw them as they ran and came chasing after them, shouting and cracking their long whips.

How those old folks ran! You would never think they were old and sick. The thought of whips curling around their legs made them move as fast as antelopes. At last, in desperation, they climbed up a tall tree.

'We won't let you down until you give up the money you stole,' shouted the villagers.

'It's all right,' whispered the skinny man to his wife. 'We'll just sit it out until they go home.'

The neighbours heard this and said: 'Here we sit until you come down.'

The old woman whispered: 'They will have to go home for supper soon, and then we will make a run for it.'

Again the neighbours heard, and they shouted: 'We shall build huts here and take it in turns to watch you.'

And this is what they did. Time went by. The skinny old man and his skinny wife sat up in the tree, and the neighbours camped out below and waited for them to get tired and come down.

At first the old couple found plenty of fruit to eat in the tree. When this was gone they picked the youngest and juiciest leaves and chewed these. Soon they had to turn to the old dry leaves. After that there was nothing left but bark, and that was bitter and nasty and little to their taste.

They had been skinny to start with. Now they were barely skin and bone. They could get little sleep at night, and their eyes sank deep into their skulls with weariness. Their teeth grew long and pointed with all that gnawing on hard bark.

One day the old man noticed that his skin was getting thick and tough. He pointed this out to his wife, and she saw that hers was the same. They looked at their hands and feet. The nails had grown long and curved, just like claws, through hanging on to the branches of their tree.

Time went by. Summer was over, and it grew very cold. One morning the old man said: 'Why, you are covered with hair!' 'So are you,' said his wife, and they were, too—long black hairs were growing over chest and back and along their arms and legs.

Still they clung to their refuge, and still the neighbours waited below for them to give up.

'That's funny,' said the old man one day. 'I've got a queer tingling feeling at the bottom of my spine.'

'So have I,' said the old woman.

They examined one another, and there, between the haunches, something was starting to stick out. It was a tail.

It was such a shock that they began to shout and scream at one another, and the sounds came out not as words but as gibbering and squeaking. Whether they could understand one another I don't know, but the villagers camping out on the ground below could make sense of none of it.

Very soon the old couple started jumping up and down. Then, using their long claws and their tails, they swung from branch to branch, and away they went, out of their tree into the next and so off through the forest, chattering and squealing. The bag of money fell out of the tree, and the puzzled neighbours picked it up and took it back to its owner.

The skinny old man and the skinny old woman stayed in the trees. In time the forest became full of

creatures like them, all chattering and squabbling and swinging by their tails. Sometimes they would come down to the village to see what they could steal. They looked a little like people and they seemed to remember that they too had once lived in huts on the ground, but whenever the villagers came too near they would shriek and run for the trees, as if they feared the sharp sting of the whip.

TIBET

# WHO IS MY NEIGHBOUR?

IN A village below the mountains of Tibet lived two neighbours. Tse-ring lived in a fine house. He had plenty of money, but he was the nastiest old miser you could find. Cham-ba's house was no better than a mud hut and he was poorer than most mice, but no one ever asked his help and went away empty-handed.

A pair of sparrows had made their nest in the roof of Cham-ba's house. They laid their eggs and a family of baby birds hatched out. One morning, one of the young birds ventured out before it was ready to fly and it fell to the ground, breaking a leg. Cham-ba found it lying there in great pain. He picked it up, made a splint out of a small twig, and tied the leg up tightly. Then he put it back very gently in its nest.

This sparrow recovered from its hurt and grew up to be a fine strong bird. As soon as it could get about alone, it flew into the fields and came back with a beakful of grain. Cham-ba was sitting outside his house, wondering what he was to do for his next meal, when the bird appeared. It dropped the grain down right under his nose, and chirped as if to say: 'This is for you. Plant it and see what happens.'

Cham-ba was amused by the bird, and thought it could do no harm to carry out its wishes. So he put the grain into the soil right outside his door.

Out of each grain sprang a tall plant. One day Cham-ba noticed that ears of corn had formed and, looking closer, he was surprised to find that tucked into each ear there was a precious stone. This was rich payment for the small kindness he had done the bird, and he quickly harvested the jewels. Next day he took them into the town and sold them for a large sum of money.

Now, see what a change there was! The poor man could afford anything he wanted, and, although he spent money wisely, no one could fail to notice that he was now a man of wealth.

Tse-ring was curious to find out the reason for this change of fortune. He therefore asked Cham-ba to call upon him and gave him a jug of strong beer. Cham-ba, who never suspected ill of anyone, readily told him the whole story.

By now the sparrows were nesting again, and one pair ventured to build in the roof of Tse-ring's fine house. Normally Tse-ring would have pulled it down without pity, but now he waited until the young birds were chirruping above his head. Then he got a ladder and climbed up to the nest. He took out one of the sparrows and dropped it on to the ground. Its leg was broken. Tse-ring tied up the damaged leg and put the bird back.

Sure enough, the sparrow, when it had grown up, went into the fields and came back with its beak full of grain. It brought this to Tse-ring and chirped as if to say: 'Plant this, and you will be rewarded for your kindness.'

That is what Tse-ring did. He waited impatiently while the grain sprouted and grew. Then, one morn-

ing, he found an enormous ear of corn. He split it open, and out stepped a big, angry man.

'Read these,' said the man, and he spread a bundle of papers in front of Tse-ring. 'These prove that you are deeply in debt to me and that I have the right to claim repayment.' And the stranger took possession of Tse-ring's house and all his wealth, and Tse-ring himself was forced to work as a servant in the house that he once owned.

Meanwhile Cham-ba continued to prosper. He was now an important man of business. It became necessary for him to go away from home for a few days to attend to his affairs, and he was worried because he had to leave behind a big sack of gold dust, and he feared that thieves would come and steal it while he was away. He asked Tse-ring to take care of it in return for a small wage, and the neighbour agreed.

Tse-ring kept opening the sack and gazing at the gold. He let it trickle through his fingers, and it felt good. At last he could resist no longer. Handful by handful he stole the gold and replaced it with sand. At last it was all gone, to the smallest grain.

Cham-ba came home and asked for his sack. His neighbour handed it over. Cham-ba opened it and looked inside.

'What is this?' he said. 'I left you in charge of a sack of gold. You have given me back a sack of sand.'

Tse-ring put on a look of great surprise. 'My friend! It has turned into this,' he stammered.

Cham-ba said no more.

In spite of the loss of the gold, Cham-ba was still a rich man, and he wanted nothing so much as to do good to his fellow villagers. Now he made up his mind to open a school which all the children of the village might attend free. Along with other parents Tse-ring sent his son to this school.

One day Tse-ring had to visit the town, and he asked Cham-ba to take care of his son while he was away. Cham-ba agreed.

Now Cham-ba had bought a parrot some time before and was teaching it to talk. While Tse-ring's son was doing his sums, Cham-ba continued the parrot's lessons.

Tse-ring returned home and came to the school to collect his son. All the children were sitting cross-legged, chanting their lessons. A parrot was clinging to its perch in the middle of the schoolroom, but there was no sign of Tse-ring's son.

'Where is my boy?' said Tse-ring. 'I hope he has been working hard.'

Cham-ba walked across the room, picked up the parrot, and handed it to him.

'What is all this?' said Tse-ring angrily. 'That's not my son. Where is he? I trusted you to take good care of him.'

Then the parrot spoke: 'My father! I have turned into this.'

Tse-ring stormed and raged, but to no effect. Cham-ba would not say a word, and the parrot went on, over and over again, until Tse-ring was nearly out of his mind: 'My father! I have turned into this.'

At last Tse-ring went home without his son or the parrot. He sat thinking for a long time, then he took the sack of gold from its hiding place, took it to Cham-ba and handed it over without a word. Five minutes later his son, miraculously changed back from a parrot, banged on his door.

MEXICO

## RABBIT AND THE GUM-BABY

MY WORD, that was a hot summer! Week after scorching week went by and not one drop of rain fell. The great rivers shrank and then dried up. Water holes turned into muddy patches of ground; then there was nothing but dust.

The animals searched everywhere for water. After a while there was only one spring left, and a fierce coyote crouched beside it, daring anyone to approach.

One day Coyote was lying there, guarding his precious water-supply. Along came a rabbit—hoppity-hop.

'Hey, Rabbit!' said Coyote. 'And how are you this fine warm day? Getting plenty to drink?' And he laughed unkindly.

'Oh, I don't do so badly,' said Rabbit. 'I sip the dew which gets trapped in the leaves of cabbages, and so I don't go short.'

'If this drought goes on much longer, there will be no dew at all. Then what will you do?'

'I shall get by,' said Rabbit.

The days went by and the sun shone hour after hour. There was silence everywhere, for even the insects had deserted the dry land. One morning Rabbit discovered that no dew had fallen. There was no way for him to relieve his thirst. He waited for his chance, and while Coyote was away from home he hopped up to the spring and drank his fill.

Towards evening he came upon Coyote.

'Hello there, Rabbit,' said Coyote. 'How is the dew these days? Plenty to keep the cabbages wet?' And he laughed until the dried grass of the prairie shivered.

'I do well enough,' said Rabbit, and off he hopped quite cheerfully.

Next day Rabbit waited until hunger forced Coyote from his post. While the fierce beast was out hunting, Rabbit went to the spring and drank and drank until his belly bulged like a little tub.

Back came Coyote, dry after the chase. He went at once to the spring, and found that the water was very low. 'That's strange,' he snarled. 'Some one must be stealing my water.' He prowled around and found that the dusty ground by the spring was covered in rabbit tracks.

'Ah, so that is where Rabbit has been getting his "dew", is it? No wonder he has kept looking so brisk and well all through the drought. Now we will make him pay for it.'

What do you think that coyote did? He poked around until he found a chunk of wood, rather bigger than rabbit-sized. He took a sharp stone and hacked the wood until he had shaped it like a baby. There was a pine tree near-by which was dripping gum, and he smeared this sticky mess all over the wooden baby. Then he set it on end so that it seemed to be guarding the spring.

Along came Rabbit, all cautious and keeping a good lookout for Coyote. That animal kept well out of sight, but there beside the spring stood the gum-baby.

'Good morning,' said Rabbit politely. 'How are you keeping? Well, I hope.'

Gum-baby replied never a word.

'That is not very nice,' said Rabbit. 'When I speak to you, I expect you to speak back to me, or I'll soon teach you a lesson in good manners. Now, I'll give you one more chance. Good morning, Gum-baby.'

Not one word came back from Gum-baby.

'I gave you fair warning,' said Rabbit, and he poked Gum-baby right in the middle with both paws.

Gum-baby tumbled over backwards, but Rabbit had stuck fast to the gum and over he went too. Both of them went—splash—into the spring. As he struggled to get himself free, Rabbit drank a lot more water than he fancied.

Then Coyote came out of hiding, and he laughed and he laughed. When he had finished, and Rabbit had at last got himself free, Coyote was so tired and so happy that he just could not wish for any further revenge. Rabbit crawled home, the wettest creature in all the prairie on that day of drought.

HUNGARY

# PRINCE OF NETTLES

THE miller's son left home to seek his fortune. He flung his bag of tools over his shoulder and tramped along the dusty road until he came to a river and on its banks a mill, lying half in ruins.

'This will do me,' he said to himself, and he set to work with hammer and saw and put it into working order.

That was a big job, to be sure. By the time he had finished he was quite worn out and so were his clothes, for they hung around him in rags and tatters. But there it was; his mill was ready, and he waited for people to bring their corn to be ground. He waited and he waited, but no-one came near the place.

What, no-one? Well, you wouldn't count a fox, who came running with the hounds not far behind. He panted: 'Find me somewhere to hide. You won't regret it.'

'Get under that sack,' said the miller, and when the hunt turned up a few minutes later he sent them off the wrong way.

'Thank you, miller,' said the fox when danger was passed. 'I'll do you a good turn too. How would you like a nice little wife?'

'A fine chance I have of that,' said the miller. 'Just look at me! No money, and only the rags I stand up in. No girl, nice or otherwise, would give me a second look.'

'We'll see about that,' said the fox, and he trotted off. He was back before long with a bit of copper in his jaws. 'Hold on to this,' he said. 'It will come in useful before long.'

Next day the fox came again, this time with a large chunk of gold. 'Put this in a safe place,' he said, and was away in a flash of his bushy tail. Two days later he returned, and now he brought a fine diamond. 'Now we won't be long,' he said. 'It is high time we did something about this wife for you. You can leave everything in my capable paws. Just give me the bit of copper.'

Away went the fox at a brisk trot and he did not stop until he came to the king's court. 'Greetings, Your Majesty,' he said. 'I hear that you have a daughter and no husband for her yet. My master, Prince Csihan, sends this small gift of copper. He is looking for a wife, and your girl might perhaps suit him.'

'Bring him along and let me have a look at him,' said the king. 'Here, take him this ring as my good-will gift.'

Back trotted the fox to the mill. 'Cheer up, miller,' he said. 'You have a new name now. You are Prince Csihan. Don't forget it. A very good name it is too, seeing that your mill garden is nothing but nettles. The king sends you this ring and invites you to visit his court to pay your respects to the princess. If you do exactly what I say, you are made. Now give me that gold. I'll take it to the king so that he will know that you are a man of substance.'

The fox was back at the palace early next day. 'Good news, Your Majesty,' he said. 'My prince is disposed to like this match, and he sends you this gold to help with the wedding expenses. He is sorry that he has no smaller change, but all his gold comes in lumps as big as this.'

'Well, well,' said the king. 'This seems to be a fine prince. He should do nicely for my daughter.'

Now the fox returned to the miller. 'Tomorrow we shall make your fortune, my fine Prince of Nettles,' he said. 'Be ready early.' And indeed next morning they set out at dawn. After a long walk they came in sight of a great castle. 'There,' said the fox. 'How does that suit you? There lives your bride.'

Then he gave the miller a long hard look. 'You had better take off those clothes,' he said. 'They are fit for nothing but burning.' And when the rags were gone,

'Into the river with you, and have a good bath.' So that is what the miller did.

'Now wait here and don't move until I send for you,' and the fox left the miller in the forest and trotted off to the king.

'Oh unlucky day!' he panted. 'We set off in state in a carriage drawn by six fine horses and with three waggons laden with gifts for Your Majesty, but robbers set on us as we came through the forest, and everything is gone. The prince himself has been stripped to his skin, and I have had to leave him hiding his shame in the woods. All he had left in the world is this diamond, and he has sent it to you for a wedding gift to his bride.'

At once the king called for a carriage and horses, and he found robes fit for a prince. Then they drove off to the forest, and the fox took the robes and found the miller cowering in the bushes. 'Here, put these on quickly,' he said, 'and for goodness sake wear them as if you are used to such finery. The king is waiting.'

When they reached the court the king took the miller by the hand. 'My dear son,' he said. 'How I grieve for your misfortune! But do not despair. Your troubles are at an end. The priest is waiting, and he will marry you to my daughter with no more delay.'

So the wedding took place, and the feasting went on for many days. The miller went about in a daze but he liked his new wife very well, and the comfort and good living were equally to his liking. He felt that he had nothing more to wish for.

But one day the princess said to him: 'Dearest, isn't it time that we went to see your kingdom? Your subjects must be longing to see their prince again.'

Well, that took the polish off the prince's pleasure! He went off very reluctantly to the stables to prepare for the journey. There was the fox, stretched out at his ease in the straw, and the miller's tears began to fall in earnest when he saw him.

'What's your trouble, my nettly prince?' said the fox.

'It's the princess,' said the miller. 'She wants to visit my kingdom. What am I to do?'

'Don't you worry. Just get ready for the journey.'

So they prepared a carriage, and loaded three waggons with all the treasure that had been given at the wedding. Then they set out.

The fox scampered on ahead. Soon he came upon herdsmen driving a great herd of oxen. 'Whose beasts are these?' he said. 'They belong to our mistress, the ogress,' they said. 'If anyone asks you,' said the fox, 'tell them that they belong to Prince Csihan.'

Then he ran on to the ogress's castle. 'Let me in quickly, mother,' he gasped.

'Lucky for you that you called me mother!' growled the huge old woman. 'Otherwise I'd have ground your bones to poppy-seed.'

'Never mind about that,' said the fox. 'I came to warn you that an army is on its way to capture you.'

'I must hide,' said the ogress.

'Come with me. I know just the place,' and the fox took her to a cave on the shores of a deep lake. 'There, wash your face here and I will return when danger is past.'

The fox ran back to the miller. 'Come on,' he said. 'Your palace is waiting.' And he led the way to the ogress's castle, where everything, although rather on the big side, was as rich and plentiful as even a princess could wish.

When the happy couple were safely asleep that night, the fox went back to the ogress. 'I heard the noise of horses,' she said. 'The army can't be far away. Isn't there somewhere safer that I can hide?'

'Come this way,' said the fox. He led her through the darkness to a cliff-top above the lake. Then he went behind her and gave her a sharp push. Into the lake she went and was drowned. The fox returned to the castle, and now there was no-one to question the right of Prince Csihan and his bride to live there.

The miller was well pleased with his good fortune. He gave a great feast to all his new neighbours and everyone was satisfied, except the fox.

'It is time I had my reward,' said the fox to himself. 'I'll sham illness and see how the prince will treat his old friend.' So that is just what he did. He lay in the hall, groaning as loudly as he could.

'What a dreadful noise!' said everyone.

'He is a nuisance,' said the prince. 'Get rid of him, someone. Throw him on the dung-hill.'

There the poor beast lay with not a friend in all the world. One day Prince Csihan passed that way. 'Hey, Prince of Nettles!' howled the fox. 'A fine prince you have turned out. Have you ground much flour lately?'

'Hush!' said the prince. 'Someone will hear you.'

'Prince Miller!' bawled the fox. 'There may be honour among princes and foxes, but none among millers.'

'Be quiet, and you shall be my best friend and companion.' And he took the fox in, and from that day fox and prince sat at the same table and ate the same food.

So they lived happily, and I dare say they are doing so still, if they are not dead.

EGYPT

# THE PRINCE AND HIS FATE

THE KING of Egypt had longed for a son over many years and, when one was at last born to his queen, he rejoiced greatly. He sent for his wise men and ordered them to look into the future. When they had studied the stars for a long time, they declared that the boy would die 'by a crocodile, or a snake, or a dog'. They could not decide which, but die he must.

The king made up his mind to cheat fate. He had a tower built far in the wilderness. Here the boy grew up in safety, enjoying every comfort except freedom to move about among his fellow men.

One day, when the prince had lived in this way for a long time, he went up on to the roof and looked out. There was a man walking along the road, and a small animal followed close at his heels.

'What is that creature?' asked the prince.

His servant said: 'Why, that is a dog.'

At once the prince felt a great longing to have just such a companion in his loneliness. The king would not hear of it. But the prince went on asking for a dog until at last the king could refuse him no longer. So a fine young dog was brought to the tower, and the young prince made much of him.

Still he was not free to go about like other people. He pestered the king to be allowed to make his own way in the world. At last the king told him what fate had in store for him, and in what danger he lay. 'What of it?' said the young man boldly. 'If I am doomed to die, I shall die, however much you protect me. Would it not be better to let me enjoy such years as the gods allow me? Please, father, set me free to seek out my fate in my own way.'

The king admired his son's brave spirit. He had the tower door flung open, and the prince came out into the world for the first time, and his dog came out with him.

Together they set their faces to the north. For days they journeyed, hunting for their food and eating what they could catch. It was a good life, and the young man and his dog lived it joyously and without care for the future.

In time they came to a land ruled over by a proud lord. In the middle of the capital city the prince saw a very tall building. It reared a hundred feet above the ground, and the only windows were at the top. The young man spoke to a passer-by and was told that in this tower lived the lord's only daughter. Here she must stay until a man succeeded in climbing to her window. Many had attempted the climb, but one by one they had fallen to their death and the girl remained a prisoner.

The prince looked up, and saw a young girl looking out. Their eyes met. He knew well what it was like to be shut in a tower. Besides, he recognized her beauty as well as her helplessness, and he made up his mind to help her. He went to the palace and spoke to the guards, saying that he was a nobleman of Egypt who had run away from home because of a stepmother's hatred. He asked to be allowed to make the climb, and the guards agreed that he should try next morning.

At dawn he went to the tower, and slowly, his hands and feet seeking out the fine cracks in the stone, he fought his way upwards until he reached the prisoner's window. She helped him over the sill and kissed him.

At first the lord was angry because his daughter had been rescued by a runaway from Egypt and not by one of the local princes. 'I will have none of him!' he shouted, and ordered the young man to be banished from the land. But the daughter held him fast in her arms, saying that she would never let him go. The lord then ordered his guards to slay the foreigner. Again the daughter defied her father, saying that she would live and die with her lover. In the end the lord saw that he could in no way break his daughter's will, and so he gave the young man his blessing. The two young people were married, and they lived in great contentment together in that land.

One day, the wife said: 'This happiness of ours must last for ever. Don't ever leave me.'

'Alas!' said the prince. 'The time must come when we have to part. At my birth my fate was written, that I should die by a crocodile, or a snake, or a dog.'

'You have a dog,' said the wife. 'Put him to death, or he may bring you to your end.'

'No,' said the prince. 'He has been a good friend to me ever since he was a puppy, and I am not afraid of him. Let us not shrink from fate, but accept what comes with a good heart.'

A time came when the prince found that he had in him a great longing to see Egypt once more. His wife would not let him go alone, and so the two set out together, each delighting in the other's company. They came at last to his father's capital city, and there they stayed secretly for a time. The people of that city were living in great dread because of a mighty crocodile which lived in the river and took tribute every day of the lives of women and children. The prince's wife was troubled when she heard this story, but the prince himself showed no fear.

One day weariness came upon the young man and he lay down to sleep, and his wife put a bowl of milk by his side so that he might drink when he awoke. Then she sat and watched over him. During the night a snake came out of a hole in the wall and crawled towards the prince, but his wife took the milk and set it down in the reptile's path. The snake drank until it was full and then lay down to sleep. The wife took a knife and slew it. The prince awoke and saw what had happened. 'See!' said his wife. 'There lies your fate!' And the two rejoiced at their escape.

A day came when the prince longed to go hunting. He knew his wife would fear for his safety, so he waited until she was busy about the house, and then he walked into the fields with his dog. The dog was wild with happiness, for he had not been hunting for months. He startled a heron which flew over the river, and the dog plunged in the water after him. The prince followed, and together they swam into deep water. Suddenly the great crocodile appeared. It took the young man by the shoulder and dragged him to its den on a reedy island.

'Look at me,' said the crocodile. 'I am your fate.'

'It is well,' said the prince. 'I am ready to face my fate,' and he bowed his head and waited for the end.

But there was a great noise of barking, and the prince's dog appeared. He at once attacked the crocodile and struck out one of its eyes. The prince took his spear and joined in the battle, and after a mighty struggle he stabbed the monster to the heart.

The dog lay dying, with his back broken by the crocodile's tail. 'Dear master,' said the dog. 'I too was your fate, but you have faced fate in all its three forms and defeated it. Live happy!'

So the prince went back to his wife and told her what had happened. 'I tried to run from my fate,' he

said. 'It was folly. I carried my fate always with me. Now I have faced and destroyed it.'

He was now free to make himself known to his royal father. The king made him and his wife welcome, and he proclaimed the young man as his heir. In his turn he came to rule the kingdom, and he did this wisely and his wife with him. Then, one day when he had grown old, his fate returned. He was walking in his garden, sad and lonely because his wife was now dead and his life seemed empty. A small snake lay in his path, and it sank its fangs into his foot. He died quickly and without regret.

KOREA

# PIGLET AND THE COW

KANG WA the judge was not content to be a widower. His wife had been in the grave barely a year when he took another, a rich widow with a grown-up daughter of her own. Oh, she was a stuck-up girl, that one, and mighty pleased with herself even if she was no beauty and neither clever nor kind.

Kang Wa already had a daughter of his own. She was a sweet girl, pretty as pear blossom, and that indeed was her name. Pear Blossom had been a happy child, with a mother who loved her dearly, and now she found herself with a harsh stepmother and a

stepsister who did all she could to make life miserable. Mother and daughter joined in bullying the poor girl, making her do all the heavy and dirty work of the house and sparing her never a kind word. They would not even call her by her real name. To them she was always 'Piglet'.

Her father was no comfort. He was such a proud man, so vain about his own importance. His main thought was to look smart and well-dressed, and Piglet spend long hours starching and pressing his coat and his shirt, so that when he went in the morning to the courts he looked like nothing so much as a pillar of snow. The only black thing about him was his tall hat, but sometimes he was in a black mood too, if Piglet had done something to anger him.

So it went on until the day came when there was to be a big festival in the city. Piglet was kept harder

than ever at work, washing and pressing clothes so that her father and his new wife should look splendid when they went to see the royal procession.

The girl worked willingly enough, hoping that if she did all her tasks well her stepmother would let her watch the festivities. Not a hope! Before the others went off in all their finery, the stepmother gave her a great bag of newly harvested rice and told her to take off the husks. When that was done, she was to fill a big jar with water from the well. The jar was not only large; it had a big crack in it so that the water ran out as fast as it was filled.

Poor Piglet! She sat down to her first task and spilled out the rice on the mat, but she could scarcely see to begin for the tears that filled her eyes.

Suddenly the air was full of the noise of wings, and in came a great flock of white doves. They settled

on her head and shoulders, her arms and hands, and they cooed and kissed her with their little beaks. Then they dropped to the ground and set to work. Beaks pecked swiftly and neatly, and in no time at all on one side rose a pile of white rice, on the other a heap of grey husks. The air was filled with their wings again as away they flew.

Well, that made life seem better to Piglet, but there was still the water to be drawn. She picked up the great jar and went to the well, not knowing how she was going to manage the leaking vessel.

She had just lowered the bucket for the first time when she heard a strange squeaking at her feet. Looking down she saw a little man, hardly up to her knee and black as soot. Indeed he seemed to be made of soot!

'Stop that boo-hooing!' said this little creature. 'There's nothing wrong that can't be cured. I am the

fire-imp, and often enough you have kept me warm by feeding the fire and clearing out the ashes. It is my turn to help you.'

He ran outside and was back in a moment with a handful of wet clay. With this he patched the jar. Then he seized the handle of the well and whirled it around. Down went the bucket and up it came brimming with water. Before Piglet had time to blink the jar was full and, what is more, all the water stayed inside.

The imp vanished without waiting for thanks, so Piglet washed herself quickly and changed into her best clothes (but these were very shabby, although spotlessly clean), and she ran out into the street in time to see the king go by with all his soldiers and ministers in their fine clothes.

Some time after this the family decided to have a day out in the mountains. This made still more work for Piglet, because they had to have all their best dresses newly washed and starched and special food prepared. The girl was fairly dropping with weariness when she finished. But could she go with the others on their holiday outing? Not she! Stepmother told her to stay at home until she had hoed the garden and weeded all the paths, and it was a very big garden too.

Off they all went, with a great deal of laughter and shouting, and Piglet went into the garden in tears. 'Moo!' came a sound from close behind her. She looked around and there stood a huge black cow. It gazed kindly at her, and I think it would have smiled if it had known how. Then it lumbered past her and began to eat. Do you know? That cow just ate up every weed in the garden and left the plants and vegetables untouched, and all the time its great hooves were crushing and tearing up the weeds that grew between the stones of the path. In ten short minutes all Piglet's work had been done for her and with no trouble at all.

The cow ambled out of the garden, and Piglet followed her into the woods. There the clever animal showed her where all the best wild fruits grew, and she feasted as she had not done since her father's second marriage.

Now, the stepsister noticed that Piglet was looking happier than usual and did not seem hungry, although they had kept her so short of food that most of the time she was half starved. Moreover there were fruit stains on her lips and hands. It did not take her long to get the whole story out of the girl.

The stepsister had a talk with her mother. The result was that next time there was a festival the stepsister said that she did not want to watch the procession, so Piglet could go instead.

That was a surprise. What Piglet did not realize was that the girl had decided to see the cow for herself and have her share of good things to eat. Well, Piglet set out, clean and smart as could be, and the stepsister went into the garden. In came the cow. It sniffed at the girl, and then set about eating all the vegetables it could get its tongue to. The stepsister shouted angrily and slapped the beast's fat sides, and it wandered out of the garden. She followed eagerly. That cow led her through brambles and nettles, rock and swamp. She tore her fine clothes, bruised her knees, tangled her hair and scratched face and arms, and finished up crying and quite worn out.

Meanwhile Piglet was having a fine time at the festival. She watched the procession, and then went into the city (for her stepmother had, surprisingly, given her some spending money) and had a good meal and saw all the sights.

She looked so pretty and happy, so neat and well mannered, that a rich young man, up from the country to see the festival, was greatly taken by her. He made inquiries and found out who she was and where she lived. Then he got a friend to call on her father and ask formally for her hand in marriage. Kang Wa had almost forgotten that he had a daughter, thinking of her only as the girl who starched his shirts. At first he tried to put the young man off with his stepdaughter, but he would have none of this. At last Kang

Wa agreed to the match, and there was a grand wedding. Piglet was Piglet no more but Pear Blossom, and didn't she look beautiful in her fine wedding gown of purest silk?

And do you know what Pear Blossom had for her chief bride-gift? Why, a clay model of a black cow! And in the courtyard of her fine new house the doves flew and cooed and ate their fill.

CANADA

# WOLFSKIN'S BRIDE

A MAN and his wife lived with their only daughter by the shores of the dark sea. All around them lay the ice and snow of the northern country. Bitter hard was the life they led, and they were often sore pressed to find enough to keep breath in their bodies.

One morning the daughter got up early and went out into the snow. Something black was lying on the white ground. She went closer and saw that it was a fine caribou, newly killed. She told her father, and together they hauled their find home. That day, and for several days afterwards, they were able to fill their bellies with good food.

In the night the daughter awoke and had a feeling that someone was in the house. She sat up and looked around in the dim light. Was that the tail of a wolf just going through the door? She could not be quite sure.

A few days later she was up early again. It had been a bitter cold night and the sea was frozen far out. On the ice lay something black. She went to look and found that it was a seal, dead but so recently that it still bled. Her father added this to his food store.

That night the girl was disturbed again and sat up in her bunk. It looked very much like a wolverine's tail that was disappearing through the door. She got up and looked outside, but nothing was stirring.

At the end of that day they were sitting down to their meal when the door opened. In came a tall young man dressed in a wolf-skin coat. 'My father told me to come for you,' he said to the girl and took her by the hand. Before she had got over her surprise and could say a word, another young man burst in. His coat was trimmed with wolverine fur. He pushed the first intruder out of the way and said: 'You may have got here first, but I'm the one she will marry.'

'She is mine,' said Wolfskin, and raised his hand to strike the other.

'Get outside, if you want to fight,' said the father, and he pushed them both out of the door. The family sat inside and listened to the sound of gasps and blows, but they did not try to interfere. After a while the noises stopped, and there was complete silence.

'It's no business of ours,' said the father, and so they all went to bed.

Next morning the girl was awake very early. She hurried outside. The marks of a struggle showed clear in the snow. Two sets of tracks led away from the house, a wolf's and a wolverine's, and there was much blood, shining bright red. The girl was afraid, but she forced herself to follow the trail until she came up to a dead wolverine, its side torn open.

She went and told her father, but again he said 'It's not our affair.'

As they were eating their meal that evening, the door opened again. This time it was an old man who came in. His coat was of wolf-skin. He said: 'My son is dying. The girl must come at once. There's no time for words.'

The father did not like it, but he was afraid to say no. So the girl put on her furs and went out. The old man gripped her hand and hurried away. As soon as they were out of sight of the house he said: 'Climb on my back and keep your eyes shut.'

She scrambled on to his shoulders and he began to run. It seemed to her that, the farther they went, the more wolf-like he became, but she could see nothing. It was dawn when they reached a low hut. He made her get down on her knees and crawl through the door. Wolfskin lay beside the fire and his mother sat by him. 'Is he alive?' said the father. 'Yes,' said the mother. 'But he needs the bride's help.'

Together the old ones undressed the girl and put new clothes on her. Then she knelt by the fire and nursed Wolfskin. He was sore wounded and as thin as a skeleton, but she fed him well and watched him day and night. In time he grew well enough to go out and hunt.

Now the young couple settled down together and very well they lived. Wolfskin went out hunting every night and every day they had fresh meat to eat. But she was never allowed to go with him, so she did not see his manner of hunting. She loved her new husband well and had no regrets for her old life.

One day they heard there was to be a dance in a village many miles away. The old people were unhappy and warned Wolfskin not to go, or at least to leave his bride at home. He would not hear of it. 'Someone wishes you ill,' they said, but he only laughed and got ready for the journey.

After travelling for a long time through snow and ice, they reached the village, where the guests were already dancing merrily. They joined in at once and danced until day was done. Then Wolfskin and his bride went to a hut to spend the night in sleep.

The bride was tired but still excited from the dancing. She went outside to cool her face, and a little girl came to her, saying: 'Granny wants you.' The bride did not want to go, but the child made such a fuss that she could not deny her. So they walked until they came to a cave. Inside there was a big pot on the fire, boiling, with something red like blood in it.

The grandmother greeted the bride kindly and said: 'Come, my dear. Take off your clothes and I will wash you.'

Well, the bride did not much like the idea, but

still she stripped and the old woman threw her clothes on a pile. Then she washed her well with the liquid from the pot, and nasty and sticky it was too. She washed the little girl in the same way. 'Now,' she said to her granddaughter. 'Throw the water away.' The little girl took the dirty water, but, instead of throwing it into the river, she poured it all over the bride.

Now see what happened! The young woman shrank and shrank until she was only as big as a child, while the little girl grew into a woman. This one at once snatched up the bride's clothes, put them on, and ran out of the cave. She went straight to the hut where Wolfskin was lodging, and he let her in without question, thinking she was his wife. When the real bride turned up later, dressed in the little girl's clothes, he just swore at her and sent her away.

Next evening, when the dancing began again, Wolfskin danced with the false bride. She danced like a wild thing, spinning and leaping until he was mad with love for her. Afterwards he took her to bed, while his true bride had to sleep in the snow, for no one would give her room.

As she lay shivering, another child, as like the first as could be, came and tugged her hair. 'Come on. Granny wants you,' said the child.

'I have had enough of grannies,' said the poor girl.

'You had better come,' said the child. 'Otherwise you will lose your man for ever.' So she got up.

They went to another cave, where there was a pot of water boiling on the fire.

'Come in, my dear,' said an old woman kindly.

'Take off those clothes now, and I will give you a good wash.' And this she did. After a while the old woman said: 'Do you know yourself?'

'I am my true self again,' said the bride, and she wept for joy.

She threw the dirty water into the river, while the old grandmother washed the clothes that had belonged to the wicked child. Then she gave the bride a dress of squirrel-skin and some shoes to wear. 'Now, listen carefully,' she said. 'Go to your husband's lodging. Take this water, in which I washed the clothes, and pour it into the false bride's ear while she lies sleeping. Then throw your dress and shoes out of doors, saying "Go home!" and they will return to me. After that, it is for you to do what is right.'

The bride did as she was told. As soon as the water touched the false bride, she became a child again. Wolfskin realized that he had a witch in bed with him, and he at once kicked her out of doors. Coming back into the house, he saw his true wife standing naked, for her dress and shoes had indeed gone home. 'Forgive me,' he said, and she took him to her heart.

Even now their troubles were not over. When they reached the river, on their homeward journey, they found that it had thawed and they could not get across. So Wolfskin made the sledge into a little boat, just big enough for his wife, and he set it to drift downstream. He himself ran into the woods.

The boat drifted down river for many days. The bride slept and ate the food she had with her, but she saw nobody. At last the sledge came to rest on the bank, and she saw that she was near her parents' home. She went in, and they gave her a warm welcome. 'But where is Wolfskin?' they asked. 'I don't know,' she replied, and she wept.

It was now nearly a year from the day that she had first seen Wolfskin, and she had a feeling that she would hear from him on the anniversary. So she waited patiently at home, and on the day, as they sat at supper, the door opened again. It was Wolfskin's father. 'Come quickly,' he said. 'My son is gravely ill. Only you can save him.'

She delayed no longer, but got up and went with him. Again he took her on his shoulders and ran with her as fast as a wolf on the hunting trail. At the hut she crawled through the door, and found her husband lying by the fire, thin and pale and breathing weakly. She took him in her arms and nursed him until he got back his strength.

So they lived together in great happiness for many years. At last, one day when they had grown old, Wolfskin called his sons around him and said: 'It is time for me to take your mother to another land. Share what we have amongst you, and live happily.'

Then he and his wife went outside the hut and knelt in the snow. At once they turned into two wolves, who ran off into the forest and were seen no more.

INDIA

# HOW THE BLACKBIRD WENT TO WAR

THERE was never in the world a happier married couple than the blackbirds. All day long they used to sit in their tree, singing fit to burst.

The king heard them. It seemed to him that a songster like that ought to be at Court, so he sent his fowler to catch the singing bird. That man was a proper fool! Instead of the tuneful blackbird, he caught the mate who couldn't sing a note. However, there it was; a mistake had been made and the lady blackbird was shut up in a cage in the king's palace.

When the blackbird found out what had happened he was very angry. He armed himself with a sharp thorn, put half a walnut shell on his head for a helmet, and strapped the dried skin of a frog around him for armour. Then he made the other half of the walnut into a drum, and he banged his drum—rub-a-dub-dum!—and declared war on the king.

He marched along the road, drumming, and who should he meet but a cat.

'Where are you off to?' said the cat.

'To fight the king.'

'I'll come too. He drowned my kittens.'

'Jump into my ear,' said the blackbird, and she did that and curled up quite comfortably.

On marched the blackbird—dub-a-dub-dum!—and he met a family of ants.

'Where are you off to?' said the ants.

'To fight the king.'

'We'll come too. He poured boiling water on us.'

'Jump in my ear,' said the blackbird, and he marched on. Very soon he came up with a rope and a club, and they too joined his army.

When he was getting near the palace, the blackbird came to a river.

'Where are you off to?' asked the river.

'To fight the king.'

'I'll come too. He made me wash out his stables.'

'Jump into my ear,' said the blackbird, and in flowed the river.

Rub-a-dub-dum! went the blackbird, and he came up to the palace gate. Bang bang bong! he went on the gate.

'Who is that?' yawned the porter.

'General Blackbird, to fight the king and win back his wife.'

The porter nearly fell over, laughing, when he saw the blackbird in all his armour. However, he led him through the palace yards to the throne room.

'What do you want?' said the king.

'My wife!' and the blackbird banged his drum boldly—dub-a-dub-dum!

'You can't have her,' said the king.

'Very well. Then you must take the consequences.' And the bird rattled his drum even louder—rub-a-dub-dum!

'Arrest that bird!' So they seized the blackbird and shut him up in the hen house.

When it was dark the blackbird said:

*'Come on, puss, and do your worst.*
*Chase those hens until they burst.'*

The cat jumped out of his ear and leapt among the hens. What a commotion! The hens scattered in all directions, clucking and screeching. Feathers flew, and one by one the cat wrung those hens' necks. Then she climbed back quietly into the blackbird's ear and went to sleep.

Next morning the king went to the hen house. There was the blackbird, singing cheerfully, and around him lay dead hens. The king was angry. 'Shut him in the stable,' he shouted, and so the blackbird was locked in with all the great horses.

When it was night the blackbird said:

*'Come out, stick; come out, rope.*
*Bind those nags in case they kick.*
*Whack them hard until they're sick.*
*Beat them till they have no hope.'*

Out jumped the rope and tied up the horses. Out jumped the stick, and it whacked those horses until there was not one left alive. Then they climbed back into the blackbird's ear and went to sleep again.

In the morning the king went to the stable. The blackbird was singing joyfully and banging his drum, and there lay all the king's fine horses.

How angry the king was! 'Put him in with the elephants,' he said. 'I have had enough of this foolery.'

So the blackbird was shut in with the elephants.

As soon as it got dark the blackbird said:

*'Now, dear friends, you swarmsome ants,*
*Wake these lazy elephants.'*

Out swarmed the ants. They crawled all over the elephants. They climbed up inside their trunks, and wherever they went they bit and stung until the great beasts could do nothing but lie down and die.

'Well done!' said the blackbird, and the ants went back into his ear for the rest of the night.

When the king went to the elephant house in the morning, he heard the blackbird singing and drumming, and there were all the royal elephants, lying dead in heaps.

'What shall I do with this wretched bird?' said the

king in despair. 'Tie him to my bed, and I'll watch him myself all night.'

So they tied the blackbird to the king's bed-head. Night came. The king got into bed but stayed awake to see what would happen. When it was quite dark the blackbird said:

*'Wake up, river, no more sleep.*
*Drown this bedroom fathoms deep.'*

Now, watch what happens.

Here comes the river, pouring out of the blackbird's ear as if there will be no end to it. The floor is awash. The bed begins to float. The king's nightshirt is soaked.

'Oh, for goodness sake!' said the king. 'Take your wretched wife and go home.'

So that is how General Blackbird won the war.

USA

## WINTER'S END

IT WAS deep winter. The land lay covered with snow and even the swift stream had frozen hard. The old man huddled over his dying fire, shivering. He longed to hear a human voice once more before death came for him, but the only sound in his lonely valley was that of wind in the trees.

Then, one morning, a fine young man came to his hut. He strode along with a light step, singing a gay song. In his hand he bore not a spear but a spray of fresh flowers.

'Come in, my son,' said the old man. 'It is many days since I last heard the sound of a voice, and I am right glad to see you. Sit down. You shall tell me all about your travels and the strange adventures you have had, and I will tell you what I have been doing, too.'

The young man flung himself down beside the fire. The old man fumbled in his bag and took out a pipe, beautifully and richly carved, and filled it with tobacco leaves. He put fire to it and handed it to his guest, who took a deep breath of smoke and blew it into the air. The old man did the same and they settled down comfortably to talk.

'First,' said the old man, 'I shall tell you what powers I have. When I send out my breath the water stand still. They become like stone.'

'When I breathe out,' said the young man, 'flowers spring up all over the meadow.'

'I shake my hair,' said the old man, 'and snow falls from the sky and covers the whole land. I speak and the leaves fall. Birds fly away and every animal hides from my sight. I tread on the ground and it becomes rock-hard.'

'I shake my long hair,' said the young man, 'and soft rain drops out of the sky and waters the earth. Plants peep out from the ground like children searching for their mothers. I sing and birds return from their homes in distant lands. I breathe over the waters and they flow again. When I walk through the woods all nature sings to greet me.'

They fell silent and sat there, both staring at the flickering flames of the dying fire. The sun had broken through the clouds and the air in the clearing suddenly felt quite warm. A song-bird began to trill from the roof. There was a soft murmur as the frozen stream began to flow again. A light breeze arose, full of the scent of newly opened flowers.

The young man stretched his limbs and smiled in the sunshine. He turned to look at his companion. The old man was lying limply beside the fire. His face had fallen in, and moisture was flowing from his eyes. As the strength of the sun grew, he seemed to shrink, until by noonday he had quite vanished, leaving only a puddle of water which quickly turned to vapour.

Where the old man had been sitting, a tiny plant sprang out of the ground. It had a delicate white and pink flower, the first herald of spring.

WALES

# A BRIDE FROM THE LAKE

THERE'S magic in lakes, especially when they lie in the heart of the mountains and the steep scree slopes sweep straight down into deep black water. Such a lake was Llyn y Fan Fach under the Black Mountain. You might expect anything to happen in a place like that, and it often did.

Sion drove his herd of small Welsh black cattle one day to the shores of the lake. While they grazed he sat on a rock by the water and gave himself up to thought. Around mid-day his stomach told him that it was time to eat the bread and cheese his mother had put up for him, but as he got it out of his pouch his eye was taken by a ripple on the water. Something was swimming out there, something bigger than any fish he had ever seen. It came nearer, and then heaved itself on to the rock close beside him. It was a woman, shimmering white and naked and with long black hair. He had never seen anyone more beautiful.

He offered her a share of his food. She took one look, shook her head and said:

*'That bread is as hard as a brick;*
*You won't tempt me with that trick.'*

Then she slipped into the water like an otter and was gone.

Poor Sion went home with his head full of thoughts of lovely water-women. He told his mother what had happened, and she advised him to take some dough in his pocket next day. Perhaps the lady would like this better than her good hard-bake.

There was no sign of the lady next day when he returned to the lake. The sky was dark and gloomy and the wind blew chill. But around noon a small break came in the clouds and as the sun shone, there she was! He held out the wet dough to her. She looked at it, smiled grimly and said:

*'That bread has never felt the fire,*
*And I'll not yield to your desire.'*

Next day he was up at the lake very early, you may be sure. This time he brought with him some

bread which had been lightly baked. He sat by the lake all day, his heart beating fast, but never sight nor sound of her there was. By evening he was feeling desperate, as well as hungry. The sunlight was fading when he took one last look across the water. It seemed to him in the dazzle that some of his cows were walking on the shimmering surface. He blinked, and there she was, sitting beside him, more lovely than ever. He held out his bread and she took it. She said:

*'That bread is just right.*
*I'll be your delight.'*

He tried to take her in his arms, but she held away. 'Wait,' she said. 'I will gladly live with you and be your loving wife, but if you should strike me three times without cause I shall go away and you will never see me again.'

'I will never strike you,' said Sion, and he meant it.

She gave him one kiss, then slipped out of his arms and disappeared into the water. Sion was beside himself with excitement and disappointment, and he jumped up and down at the lake edge like a mad thing.

Then the surface rippled again, and out of it rose a tall man, stately in his royal robes and with a long white beard. After him came two lovely women, also in long robes and each in every feature like the other.

'You wish to marry my daughter,' said the man. 'So you shall, if you can tell her from her sister.'

Sion looked and looked. They were equal in beauty, in colour and in hair and skin. How could he tell which was his bride?

Then one of the women moved her foot. She twitched one toe, so slightly that it could scarcely be seen, but Sion guessed at once that she was telling him, almost as clearly as in words, that she was his love.

He stepped forward and took her by the hand. 'You have chosen aright,' said the old man. 'She is yours. She shall not come empty-handed. As many sheep and cattle and goats and horses as she can count without drawing breath she shall have as dowry. But if you strike her thrice without cause, she will come back to me and her dowry with her.'

So Sion took her home. He now became a man of wealth, and his grazing beasts spread far and wide over the mountain. He loved his strange wife dearly and she him, and not many years had passed before they had three fine sons.

A day came that they were invited to a christening. When it was time the wife made all sorts of excuses because she did not want to go. Sion kept his patience, but still she would not budge. 'It is too far,' she said. 'I am tired and cannot walk.'

'Ride then,' he said. 'Your horse is in the field. Bring it here and I will put saddle and bridle on it.'

'I want my gloves,' she said. 'Fetch them for me.'

He found the gloves, but now time was running short and so was his patience. 'Let us be going,' he said, and he tapped her on the shoulder with the gloves.

'That is one blow,' she said. 'Take care. You have only two more.'

The next year passed happily enough, and then there was a day when they were asked to a wedding. It was a jolly occasion and there sat all the guests, drinking and eating and laughing. Suddenly the wife burst into tears. The husband leaned over and touched her on the arm, saying: 'Whatever is the matter?'

'How can I help weeping, seeing two young people beginning a life of troubles together? And as for you, husband, you must look to your own troubles, for you have struck me twice. You have only one more chance.'

He made up his mind to take more care in the future, and he did, too. For many years they lived most contentedly together, each growing fonder of the other as time passed. The children grew up and showed signs of wisdom. The mother taught them all her lore and showed them what healing lay in many plants and herbs.

Then a neighbour died and the family went to the funeral. They were all standing at the graveside, weeping, when the wife broke into peals of happy laughter. Sion was shocked. 'Quiet, my love!' he said, turning and grasping her arm. 'Why do you break in upon their grief?'

'Why should I not laugh,' she said, 'seeing that the dead have gone into the light and left their burdens behind them? But you, dear husband, have struck your last blow, and we must part.'

She walked away sadly, whistling to her cattle as

she went, and her sheep and cows and goats and horses turned and followed her. Even the calf which had been slaughtered that morning and hung up for their dinner came down from its hook and joined the procession. They went on together, up the mountain and to the shores of Llyn y Fan Fach. They walked into the water and disappeared from sight. Last to go was the team of oxen that was working at the plough. Beasts and plough went together, and left a deep furrow to the water's edge.

Sion went sadly home with his three sons. He never saw his lovely wife again. The boys grew up and, through the wisdom she had taught them, they became famous throughout Wales for their skill in curing sickness and mending broken bones.

AUSTRALIA

# THAT WICKED CROW

AH, THAT old crow! He was a bad one and no mistake. He flew about Australia looking for trouble, and if he couldn't find any, why, he just made some for himself.

None of the other birds liked him, and no wonder. They used to chase him away as soon as they set eyes on him, but then he took to calling each one 'Brother-in-law'. You can't prove a relationship like that very easily. So whichever bird it was—whether bower-bird or emu or eagle—usually let the crow get away with it. Suppose it really was his brother-in-law!

One day Crow flew to a part of the coast where he had never been before, and below him he saw a great flock of pelicans. Down drifted Crow, like a small black cloud bringing bad weather—or trouble of some kind anyway—with him.

One of the pelicans looked up and blinked at him. 'Greetings from me and my kinsmen, brother-in-law,' said Crow.

'Those are strange words from a stranger,' said the pelican. 'I have never seen you before.'

'It is a long story,' said Crow. 'In my country it is common knowledge that we crows and you pelicans are related. A brother of my great-great grandfather married the sister of your grandmother's grand-aunt, and that, according to our laws, means that we are brothers and share all things in common. See! It is all written down here.' And crow held up a stick on which many signs had been cut.

The pelican had never learnt to read, so he had no choice but to believe Crow. 'Come along,' he said. 'Follow me and I will take you home.' So the pelican hopped along and Crow followed, but he soon started to groan as if in pain and pretended to have a bad limp in one leg.

'What's the matter?'

'Oh, it is nothing,' said Crow bravely and limped worse than ever. 'It is just that on my way I got into a fight with a tribe of emus. Believe me, I gave as good as I got, but in the end the emu chief tricked me out of my guard and stabbed me in the ankle with his spear. After that I had to fly for my life or they would surely have torn me to pieces.'

Crow could not tell the truth, try as hard as he liked—and he wasn't trying hard! But the pelican was impressed and he helped Crow to reach the ground where the tribe was camped. All the pelicans gave him a friendly welcome, fed him with the best of their food, and then let him sleep in their favourite roosting place.

Crow slept deeply that night and well into the morning, for he was tired and his belly was full. When he awoke the sun was high. 'What's this?' he said to himself. 'I never lie abed so late. That wretched pelican must have put a spell on me. 'I'll give him "brother-in-law"! He will be sorry he played

such a trick on me.' And in no time at all, that crow had worked himself into a passion against the kind pelican.

Crow jumped up and looked about him. There was not a pelican in sight. There were tracks everywhere, however, and he followed these to a lagoon. The whole tribe was there, some of them fishing, some swimming, some just lying gossipping on the banks, but all happy in the warm sun. Crow watched them, and the happier they became the more his hatred grew.

'How can I harm them most?' he muttered. He noticed that there were no babies in sight, so he poked around, looking for them. As he came to a tall gum-tree he heard the sound of chirping and saw that the mothers had hidden their young in a fork, high enough to be safe from enemies.

'That's what I'll do!' said Crow. 'I'll get those babies down and eat the lot. They will make a tasty meal, and won't the mothers be upset? They will be sorry that they offended me. It will teach them not to tangle with Crow.'

First he tried to fly up to the fork, but when that failed he thought he would scramble up the trunk, but it was smooth as glass and he just couldn't get a grip.

'Right! I'll chop the tree down.' He hurried back to the camp and stole an axe from the pelicans' store. 'Down it comes!' he shouted and swung the axe, but it twisted in his grip and nearly broke his wing.

'I'll burn it down.' He took a torch and lit it at the camp fire, but when he put it to the tree it just smoked and flickered and then went out.

'I know. I'll call up the forest-spirits.' So Crow began to sing an evil song. Out of the forest crept a crowd of tiny creatures which danced around the tree. 'Grow, tree! Grow!' sang Crow. Every time he said 'Grow' the spirits threw their boomerangs into the air and the tree grew upwards. By the time Crow had finished his song it was so tall that the baby birds and their refuge could scarcely be seen from the ground.

'That will serve those pelicans right,' gloated Crow, and he hid himself and waited to see what would happen.

Before long a carpet-snake and his mate came to the foot of the tree. He had heard the noise made by the pelicans at their fishing and had decided that a few unguarded baby birds would do very well for dinner. But when he looked up he realized that the birds were far beyond his reach.

Crow just couldn't keep quiet. 'See what I did,' he boasted. 'I showed those pelicans I am not to be trifled with. I forced the spirits to make the tree grow, and now nobody will ever get those babies down.'

'You stupid bird!' hissed the snake. 'It was bad enough wishing to harm the pelicans who had done you no harm. Now you have done me out of my dinner, and that is far worse. If I get my coils around you I'll teach you better manners.' And the snake and his mate wriggled away angrily into the forest.

By now the pelicans had finished their fishing, and the mothers came to collect their babies. What a commotion they made when they saw how high the tree had grown. They screamed and wailed until there was no animal for miles around which did not know of their troubles. From every side came kangaroos and goannas and opossums and all the other beasts of forest and grassland, all swarming to the tree. There were good climbers among them, but not one could reach those babies.

The blue wren, smallest of all birds, watched them for a time. Then he said to his wives: 'Those great creatures are quite helpless. Wait here while I go and fetch the woodpecker.' So he flew for miles through the woods until his little wings were weary, and at last he came up with the woodpecker.

'You are needed at the lagoon, old friend,' said the wren. 'Those poor clumsy pelicans are going to die of grief if nothing is done for them, and all the other animals are helpless. Follow me.' And they flew back together.

Everyone was making too much noise to notice the two birds. 'Fetch me the kangaroo,' said the woodpecker, and the wren went and whispered in his ear: 'The woodpecker wants a word with you. Come quietly.'

The woodpecker told the kangaroo to get everyone to stand well back from the tree and shut their eyes. When every animal had obeyed the woodpecker went to work. Without any fuss he flew up the tree, tied the first of the babies to his back with a strip of vine, and brought it safely to the ground. He repeated this until all the babies were tucked at the kangaroo's feet. Then the woodpecker flew back to his home in the forest with not a single word to anyone.

The kangaroo called out: 'Open your eyes.' Weren't those mothers pleased to see their babies sitting quietly on the ground? They rushed forward and nearly smothered them with kisses and cuddles. But when they remembered to thank the rescuer, he was not to be seen. He and his friend the wren wanted no fuss; their pleasure was all in helping their neighbours without thought of reward.

As for Crow, when he saw his 'brother-in-law' coming towards him with that great beak uplifted, he remembered that he had a job to do in a far-off part of Australia. Off he flew at top speed and he took good care never to return to the pelicans' camping ground.

PAPUA NEW GUINEA

# IN THE LAND OF THE DEAD

THIS MAN, he was no great chief. He had no fame as a warrior, neither owned he great wealth. In one thing only did he rise above his fellows; he loved his wife.

She died, and for a time his grief was too great for words. At last he arose from the bed on which he had lain weeping for many days, and began to prepare the death feast.

Now it was the custom of his people that the meat of the cuscus should be served to the elders at such a feast. So the man called his dog and they went hunting. Before long he roused one of these creatures from its tree-roost, and he made his kill quickly and hung the body on a tree until it was needed. A second was soon added. Yet another was wanted to satisfy the hunger of the mourners, so he went on with his chase.

A third cuscus ran and the dog was close behind. The animal took refuge in a hole in the ground. When the man reached the place, he found that his dog had followed the prey. Fearing that he might lose his beast, which was very dear to him, he heaved away a great stone which lay half across the hole and looked down.

It seemed to him that he could see trees growing in the darkness below. He too went into the hole and climbed deep down into the earth. In time he came upon his dog, and he picked it up and made much of it. Then he looked around.

He had come into the land of the dead. During the day their bones lay asleep, but at night strength came back into them and they could walk about. First of those who rose up was the man's wife, for she was but newly come to that country. She saw her husband and ran joyfully to him, thinking that he too must have died and was here to keep her company. She clasped him by the arm, but when she felt his warmth and saw the blood colouring his skin she said: 'Why are you here? You are not yet one of us.'

He told her how he came to be in that place.

'Hold the dog tight and keep him quiet,' she said. 'I will find some safe place to hide you, for if the dead discover you they will be jealous and will surely destroy you.'

The man did as he was told, and lay in hiding, watching as the time came for those long dead to arise. The bones that littered the ground slowly gathered together and became whole skeletons. Then those of the dead who had the skill began to beat upon drums, and the rest danced. The man would have been sorely afraid, but he held his wife close in his arms and this kept fear at bay.

After a time the wife said: 'You must not stay any longer. They will soon tire of their dance, and then you will be found and killed. Come now, while they are busy. I will show you the way back to your own place.'

'How can I bear to go?' said the man. 'Have I not found you again?'

'Go, now,' she said. 'But, if you dare, return to me in three days, and I shall be waiting.'

So he picked up his dog in his arms and she led him away. But, as he went he noticed how, in the land of the dead, all sorts of fruits and herbs grew just as they did on earth, but bigger and finer. He put out his hand in passing and plucked a lime. It cried out as he pulled it from the tree, and at once the dead abandoned their dancing and came racing after him, a fearful sight! His wife hurried with him to the entrance and pushed him out into the upper world, just as their bony hands were about to seize him.

He got home, scarcely able to breathe for fear. Yet in three days he went back to the hole in the ground, for his love of his wife was greater than his fear. But the dead had sealed the entrance with a huge rock, and try as he would he could not shift it. So he saw his wife no more in this life, and since that day no man has gone living into the land of the dead.

PORTUGAL

# THE DANCING PRINCESS

A SOLDIER was coming home from the wars, and although all he had for pay was a sack of oranges he marched along merrily enough. But what was this? Two men giving one another mighty thumps with their fists.

'Hey! What are you fighting about?'

'What indeed! Father is dead, and all he left us was this cap. We both want it.'

'What a bother about an old cap.'

'Ah!' said one of the men. 'It's not just a cap. Put it on and say "Cap, cap, cover me" and you become invisible. Isn't that worth a fight?'

'See here,' said the soldier. 'I will hold the cap and throw this orange as far as I can. The one who gets it first shall have the cap.'

That seemed a good idea. So the soldier threw the orange a tremendous distance, and the two men raced after it. Our soldier wasted no time. He put the cap on his own head and said: 'Cap, cap, cover me.'

Back came the men, panting, but where was the soldier? And where the cap? They had been properly fooled.

The soldier went on his way, and before long he came up with two other men who were hitting one another just as fiercely.

'What's this about?'

'Why, father has died and left a pair of boots between us, and so we are fighting to see who should have them.'

'Why make a fuss about a pair of old boots?'

One of the men said: 'These are not just any old boots. Put them on and say "Boots, take me here" or "Take me there", and you will get wherever you want as fast as light.'

'I'll tell you what,' said the soldier. 'Give me the boots to mind. Then I will throw this orange as far as I can. Chase after it, and the first to reach it shall have the boots.'

This time the soldier threw the orange even farther. While the men were racing after it he pulled on the boots and said: 'Boots, take me to the city.' When the men got back, there was nothing left for them to fight about.

Now, see our soldier in the city. Everyone was

talking about the news from the palace. The king had one beautiful daughter. Every night she went to bed, and every morning she had managed to wear out seven pairs of slippers, and, what is more, these were made of iron. How did she do it? That is what the king wanted to know, and he had just proclaimed that any man who gave him the right answer should have the princess for his bride.

That sounds just the job for me, thought the soldier. I'm a bold fellow, and, besides, these little goods of mine should come in useful.

So he went to see the king. 'Try if you like,' said His Majesty, 'but I don't give much for your chances. You can have three nights. If you haven't found the answer then, you will leave your head behind when you leave.'

'That is fair,' said the soldier. So all that day he spent in the palace, eating and drinking and with servants to run his errands. Then at nightfall he was taken to the princess's room where a cot had been put up for him. He settled down and the princess brought him a good-night drink. He drained it and was soon snoring. No wonder, for the princess had put a sleeping draught in it.

Next morning seven pairs of worn-out slippers lay on the floor and the princess was looking tired. 'Well, what's the answer?' said the king. The soldier had nothing to say. 'Two days left!' said the king. The soldier said cheerfully: 'I'm not bothered.'

Another day passed. When it was night the soldier settled down in bed again and the princess brought him his drink. Next morning he awoke refreshed, but

the princess was tired as ever and seven pairs of slippers were worn to pieces.

'What's the answer?' said the king at breakfast.

'I have no idea,' said the soldier.

'One day left!'

'I'm not bothered,' said the soldier, but he was.

All that day, while he was eating and drinking and having a good time, the soldier puzzled over his problem. It was strange, he thought, that he was sleeping so deeply. Soldiers are usually on the alert, even in their sleep. Could it be that the princess was being too kind in bringing him his nightly drink?

'Drink deep,' said the princess that night, but the soldier only pretended to drain his cup. Then he lay down and snored, but his eyes were not quite shut.

At the stroke of midnight the princess got out of bed and put on her cloak. The soldier pulled on his cap under the blanket and whispered: 'Cap, cap, cover me.' Then he got up boldly, because the princess could no longer see him. He pulled on his boots and said: 'Boots, follow the princess.'

There was a carriage at the palace door, and the princess got in. The soldier followed unseen. They drove through the dark streets down to the harbour where there lay a ship all decorated with banners. The princess and the soldier went on board, and at once the ship sailed away to a distant land of giants.

On landing the princess was challenged by a sentry. 'I am the Princess of Harmony,' she said. 'Pass, Princess of Harmony and escort!' bellowed the sentry. 'What can he mean?' said the princess to herself, for it seemed to her that she was on her own. Twice more she was challenged, and each time the sentry let her pass, using the same words.

Still wondering, the princess reached a great palace where a ball was in progress. The soldier saw that all the guests were giants, and the biggest of all was the princess's lover. The soldier stood unseen in a corner and watched while the princess joined in the dancing.

She wore out a pair of iron slippers with each dance. As they fell to pieces she threw them away, and the soldier picked them up and put them in his knapsack.

After seven dances the princess was tired, and she went to talk with her lover. But just as they went to sit down, the soldier snatched their chairs from under them and they rolled on the floor. The princess and the giant were amazed, but they could not find out what had happened.

'Bring me my book of magic,' shouted the giant, and a slave came running with a big book. Before he could hand it to his master, the soldier snatched it from him and gave him such a sharp slap in the face that he tumbled over backwards. The soldier stowed the book away in his bag.

By now it was time to go home. The princess went to her ship, but the soldier simply said: 'Boots, take me home,' and there he was, in the palace.

By the time the princess got back, he was snoring in earnest.

'What's the answer?' said the king next morning at breakfast.

'I just can't say,' said the soldier.

'Your time is up,' said the king, and he sent for the executioner.

As the soldier was being led to his death, he asked the king for one last favour.

'It is agreed,' said the king.

'Send for the princess. I have something to say to her.'

The princess came, wondering.

'What if I say the princess went out at midnight?'

'It is a lie,' said the princess.

'What if I say that she went in a carriage and then in a ship and sailed to the land of the giants where she attended a ball?'

'That is a lie.'

'What if I say that she danced seven dances and wore out a pair of iron slippers in each?'

'That is a lie.'

'And what if I say that she went to whisper with her lover, but her chair was snatched from under her, and she and her lover rolled on the floor and were made to look foolish?'

'That is a lie.'

'But what if I say that the princess's lover sent for a book of magic and it vanished into air?'

'It is a lie,'

But the princess had turned very pale.

'But what if I say that the book is here, and so are the slippers?'

'It is true,' said the princess, and she wept.

'I am glad that everything is cleared up,' said the king. 'Will you have the princess for your wife, or would you rather have a wagon-load of gold?'

The soldier liked the princess well enough, but gold might be more use to a fellow whose ways were over-rough for palace life. Besides, he did not care to share his wife with giants. So he took the gold and lived very well for many years.

ISRAEL

# TOBIAS GOES ON A JOURNEY

A HARD life had old Tobit. He had been dragged from his home in Israel and forced to live in exile among foreigners and enemies, and they made a mock of him because he lived only to do good.

Time went by and he was brought very low. All his wealth had gone. Even his life was in danger because he did not hesitate, when he saw evil being done, to disobey the laws of the king himself. Then, one warm night, he decided to take his bed into the open air and sleep there. In the early

morning, as he lay there, birds flew over and their droppings fell into his eyes. He awoke and found that he had gone blind. No longer could he see the sun and the moon and the faces of Anna his wife and Tobias his son.

In his despair Tobit remembered that his cousin, who lived in a distant city, owed him money. So he called his son to him and said: 'Tobias, you must go to the city and seek out my kinsman. Tell him that you come from Tobit to collect his debt, and he will give it to you.'

'I will go gladly,' said Tobias. 'The journey will be an adventure, and as for the money, perhaps we shall be able to pay a clever doctor to bring back your sight.'

'I have no hope of that,' said Tobit. 'But go to the market and hire a servant to go with you. Find a strong young man who can fight off any bandits and keep you safe through the journey.'

Tobias thought he was well able to look after himself. Besides, he had his dog for company. However, he did what he was told. In the market-place many men waited to be hired, but one stood head and shoulders above the rest. Tobias went to him and said: 'Will you come with me to the city to collect a debt?'

The big man looked down at him, smiled and said: 'I will.'

Tobias said: 'What is your name?'

'Call me Raf,' said the tall man.

'Very well,' said Tobias. 'We shall set out at dawn tomorrow.'

So, next day, Tobias and Raf started their journey in the early light. Anna cried to see her son going away, for he had never been anywhere without her, but Tobit laughed and said: 'Stop that weeping, woman. He will soon be back. See what a reliable servant he has. He will run into no trouble with Raf beside him.'

The two men walked all day, and Tobias's dog ran to and fro, travelling twice as far as they did in his excitement. Towards evening they came to the banks of a great river. Tobias was tired and dusty from the road, so he threw off his clothes, jumped into the water and splashed about, and the dog went with him.

Suddenly there was a disturbance in the water, and a great fish appeared, its mouth wide open showing many sharp teeth. The dog barked wildly, and Tobias struggled towards the bank.

'Stay where you are,' shouted Raf. 'Grab it by the gills.'

Tobias was frightened, but he did what he was told, and after a struggle he managed to haul the fish on to dry land. It leapt about for a while and then gasped its last breath.

'Open it with your knife,' said Raf. And when this was done: 'Take out the heart and liver and gall and put them in your knapsack.'

Tobias did this. Then they made a fire and cooked the rest of the fish, and it made them a good supper. Even the greedy dog had enough to eat.

'Why did we keep the fish's offal?' said Tobias next day as they went on their way.

'It may come in useful,' said Raf, and he would say no more.

In the afternoon they reached a fine big house.

'Knock at the door and tell them who you are,' said Raf.

Tobias went through the gate. In the garden he met a beautiful young woman who greeted him with a friendly smile.

She took him to her father, and Tobias said: 'Greetings. I am Tobias, son of Tobit of Nineveh.'

The father jumped up joyfully and kissed him. 'Dear old Tobit!' he said. 'He is my kinsman and my friend.'

So they sat and talked, and Tobias told him the reason for his journey.

'Why, this is no problem,' said the man. 'Your father's cousin is mine too and I know him well. Your servant can go to him with a note from me and bring back the money. Meanwhile you must stay here. I see few travellers, and there is none more welcome than your father's son.'

They talked for a long time. Tobias took courage and confessed how much he liked the look of the daughter, for in truth he had lost his heart to her at first sight.

The father sighed. 'Ah, yes,' he said. 'Sara is a beautiful girl, but she has one great trouble. Seven times she has been married to good young men, but each time, on the wedding night, a demon has come and strangled the husband.'

'I am not afraid,' said Tobias. 'I would gladly marry her and fight the demon afterwards.'

The father was not happy, but Tobias's love gave him courage and he would take no refusal. Sara too was very happy to accept this eighth bridegroom, and in the end the father gave way. He wept, because he had taken a great fancy to the young man, but he gave his blessing, and the two were married without delay.

Before the bridal pair went to their room, Raf took Tobias aside.

'Take the heart and liver of the great fish,' he said. 'Put them in a dish and before you go to sleep set fire to them.'

Tobias did this, and a dreadful smell it made, too. Happily the wind blew away from the house, and the air in the bridal chamber remained sweet.

The demon, hurrying to claim his latest victim, caught the smoke full in the face and it nearly choked him. He took one more breath and then flew away as fast as his wings could take him and did not stop until he got to Egypt.

Tobias and Sara heard his scream and knew that they were safe.

In the morning the father got up early and took a spade to dig a grave in the garden, for he was sure that Tobias must be dead. But when he went to the chamber to get the body he found Tobias and Sara sleeping peacefully.

Well, that was a happy day. They had a wedding feast and enjoyed it so much that they kept it up for two whole weeks. At the end of that time Raf left his master and went on alone with a message to the kinsman. This man not only paid his debt but came back with Raf to bless the new bride and groom.

The time came for Tobias to return home. The father was sad and begged him to stay longer, but Tobias was eager to see his father again. The father gave him horses and cattle and many other rich gifts, and so Tobias and Sara, Raf and the dog set out on their homeward journey.

When they were nearly home Raf said to Tobias: 'Have you still got the gall from the great fish?'

'It is here,' said Tobias.

'When your father raises his face to you, rub the gall into his eyes.'

So they came home, singing and laughing, and Tobit and his wife heard them on the road. Anna ran along the path, laughing and weeping all at once, and flung her arms around her son and they kissed. But Tobit, moving in darkness, tripped over the doorstep and stumbled. He would have fallen on his face, but Tobias caught him and quickly rubbed his eyes with the gall. 'I bring hope, father,' he said.

The old man's eyes flowed with happy tears, and they washed the gall into the farthest corners of his eyes. The scales covering them peeled away, and he could see. There stood his fine young son Tobias. There was big Raf and the dog. But who was this lovely young girl?

What a story there was to be told when they got into the house! It took a long time, but at last every adventure was told and Tobit's troubles had peeled away like the coating of his eyes.

Raf was sitting in a corner, apart from the happy family.

'Have you paid him his wages?' said Tobit.

'Not yet,' said Tobias. 'He deserves all we can give him, for without his advice I should have been lost twice over.'

So the two went to Raf, and Tobit said: 'Take three times what is due to you and go with our gratitude.'

Raf got up and stood looking down on them.

'Come outside,' he said quietly, and when they were in the open air he went on: 'What I have done, I did for my Master, who does not pay in gold and silver. I have done it for your sake, old Tobit, for you are a good man, and your son is a brave boy. Now I must return to my Master. I am Raphael, one of the seven angels who go in and out before the throne of God.'

Tobit and Tobias fell on their knees and hid their faces. When they looked up again he was gone, and they saw him no more.

USA

# B'ER RABBIT IS AN UNCLE

NO-ONE would call B'er Rabbit and B'er Wolf the best of friends, but now and again they would get together over some business in which each saw some advantage to himself.

For instance, one day they chased a cow into a corner of the meadow and milked her, kick as hard as she might, and then they churned the milk and made it into best butter. They packed this into a wooden keg and buried it in a secret part of the wood.

Going home afterwards, each swore faithfully that he would not touch the butter, or even take a walk along the road to the wood, until both of them were ready to eat that butter.

Well now, old B'er Rabbit, he just couldn't stop thinking about the butter, how soft it was and what it smelled like. He remembered his promise all right, but that belly of his had a very bad memory.

B'er Wolf was sitting by his front door one morning, wondering what the day would bring him for dinner. Along the road came B'er Rabbit, running like he had a mighty big appointment.

'Hey!' said B'er Wolf. 'Where are you off to?'

'Can't stop,' panted B'er Rabbit. 'I've just heard that my sister's had a baby girl, and I can't wait to see her.'

'What are they going to call her?' shouted B'er Wolf after B'er Rabbit's back.

'Jes'-Begun!'

'That's a queer name,' thought B'er Wolf, but he said nothing.

What did that B'er Rabbit do but run straight into the wood and dig up the keg with his strong forepaws. He helped himself to a good share of butter and buried the rest very carefully.

It wasn't above a couple of weeks before B'er Rabbit was racing by again.

'Not another baby!' called B'er Wolf. 'What's the name this time?'

'Goin'-Fast!'

'I just can't make out these rabbit names,' thought B'er Wolf.

By this time B'er Rabbit had got the taste of that butter well into his mouth, and he couldn't settle until he made another visit to the wood. B'er Wolf saw him running past.

'Now where are you going so fast?'

'That sister of mine, she's been busy again. It's a boy rabbit this time, and I really must have a look at him.'

'What's his name?'

'Las'-Scraps!'

'Now what sort of a name is that?' thought B'er Wolf. 'I shall never understand those rabbits.'

That B'er Wolf, he was mighty strong in paw and jaw, but he was sure weak in the head. He still didn't suspect anything. His wife said:

'I'd keep my eye on that rabbit if I was you. Not even a rabbit can have babies that fast. It's my belief he's up to no good.'

So, before B'er Rabbit's sister could have another baby, B'er Wolf proposed that they should dig up the keg. B'er Rabbit didn't say a word until they had got into the wood. Then he started to roll on the ground and groan like he was in dreadful pain.

'What's your trouble?' said B'er Wolf.

'It's my belly,' moaned B'er Rabbit. 'It's hurting something awful. I guess I got to see the doctor right away.' And he limped away until he was out of sight, and then he ran for his life.

Well, B'er Wolf dug up the keg and pulled off the lid, and what did he find inside? Just about nothing at all. B'er Rabbit had eaten all the butter, right down to Las'-Scraps!

Of course, B'er Wolf did his best to catch B'er Rabbit and teach him a lesson or two, but he just couldn't get near him. Every time B'er Rabbit scampered off, shouting: 'Your father's a booby. Your mother's a booby. Your sisters are boobies, and your brothers are boobies. But you're the biggest booby of the lot. Go and milk the bull next time, but do it on your own!'

SCOTLAND

# FAR HAVE I SOUGHT YE

THERE was a king and he had three daughters. Little there was to choose between the two eldest, for they were both as ugly as they were stiff-necked. The youngest? Why, she was prettier than most pictures and sweet-natured with it. Her father loved her best of all—and why wouldn't he?—and she was the joy of all the people.

One night the three were talking, as girls will, about marriage.

'I'll have none but a king,' says the first. 'Nothing lower than that will be good enough.'

'I'll be satisfied with a prince,' says the second, 'just so long as he is rich and handsome.'

The youngest says: 'What a fuss! You two are so proud; if you lift your noses any higher you will fall over backwards.'

'Who will you marry, then?' say the others.

'Me?' says the pretty girl. 'Oh, I'm not bothered. If the Red Bull o' Norroway were to ask me, I'd have him, and pleased too.'

Well, it was nought but a joke, and they all took it for nothing more. But next morning, just as they were sitting down to eat, there was the most fearsome noise outside, and what do you think it was? Why, the Red Bull of Norroway, come to collect his bride! That was a sight to see. He was three times bigger than common bulls, his eyes flashed fire, and his bellowing shook the earth.

You may guess that the king was not eager to see his favourite daughter going off with such a creature. First he tried playing a trick. He persuaded the woman who looked after the palace hens to climb on the bull's back. Off lumbered the bull till he came to the duck pond, and there he tossed the poor hen-wife into the muddy water. Then back he came, roaring worse than ever. Three times the king tried to pass off one of the servants as his daughter, but each one ended up in the duck pond.

There was nothing for it but to let the youngest princess go. Her joke had taken a bad turn, but she was as brave as she was pretty. She scrambled up on to the bull's back and waved cheerfully to her family as he galloped away.

They journeyed all that day, passing through dark forests and across harsh deserts. Many savage beasts they saw, but none so fierce or so hungry that it felt like attacking the great bull. Towards evening they came to a castle where there were lights and the sound of music. The lord of the castle came himself to greet them, and if he was surprised to see such a lovely young girl with such a very ugly bull he was too well-mannered to say anything.

So they went inside where a large company of lords and ladies were dancing and making music. The newcomers were made welcome.

The princess slipped lightly from the bull's back. In the bright light of the hall she noticed that there was a sharp thorn sticking in the bull's side. She pulled it out, as gently as she could, and now what follows? The bull vanished, and in its place there stood as handsome and splendid a young prince as you could imagine. He dropped to his knees before her, kissed her hand, and thanked her for breaking the enchantment that had bound him in a bull's hide.

Everyone crowded round the two, laughing and cheering. The princess's eyes filled with tears of happiness. She wiped them away, then looked up. He had vanished! The whole company searched the castle through for many hours, but they found nothing to show that he had ever been there.

Had it been a dream, or a fancy woven by some cruel wizard? The princess refused to believe it. She would seek him, through all the world if need be. So she set out on her quest, alone, and wandered through the wilderness for many days and weeks.

One evening, when her heart was at its lowest for misery, weariness, and hunger, she caught sight of a light shining faintly through the trees. She walked towards it and came to a little cottage. The old woman who lived there invited the princess inside and gave her food and her own bed for the night.

Next morning the old woman gave her three nuts. 'Keep these,' she said. 'Crack them not when you are in distress, nor when you are in danger, nor when you are faint with hunger. But when your heart is like to break and break and break again, then open the nuts.'

So she sent the princess on her way.

She had now left the wilderness behind and was among other folk. Many fine lords and ladies rode past her, throwing up mud and dust with their horses' hooves. They laughed and talked merrily together, for they were going to a wedding. She saw others, carrying rich gifts and food. They too were to be guests at the wedding, and the groom was the Duke of Norroway. She followed them and came to a fine castle.

What a bustle there was! Cooks and dressmakers and maids and grooms ran in all directions, frantic to complete their tasks before the wedding-day.

Suddenly horns were heard, and a hunting party rode up to the castle. Some one shouted: 'Way for the Duke of Norroway!' Here came a handsome young prince with a fine lady at his side.

Now the princess's heart was like to break and break and break again, for she knew the Duke. It was her own lost love. She went into a quiet corner and broke the first nut. Inside there was a tiny woman, no bigger than her thumb-nail. The little creature was combing wool as fast as fast. The princess hid the wee wifie in her cloak and went into the castle. She asked to speak to the bride and was shown to her chamber. When the bride saw the wee wifie she would not be content until she had her for herself. She would give anything in exchange.

'You shall have her,' said the princess, 'if you will put off your wedding for one day and let me enter the duke's chamber tonight.'

The bride agreed. That night, with the duke fast asleep and knowing nothing, the princess went to his chamber. She sat down by his head and sighed and sang:

*'Far hae I sought ye,*
*Near am I brought t' ye;*
*Dear Duke o' Norroway,*
*Will ye no' turn and speak t' me?'*

He turned in his sleep and muttered, but he did not wake up. She sang her song again and yet again, but he never waked.

Next day she broke the second nut, and inside was a little woman, no bigger than her thumb-nail, who was spinning thread as fast as fast. You may be sure that the bride wanted this wee wifie too, and she readily agreed to put off the wedding again. So the second night the princess went in to the sleeping duke and sang her sad song, but still he slept on.

On the third day she broke the last nut. In it was a little woman, no bigger than her thumb-nail, who was reeling thread as fast as fast. Again the bride wanted this toy and minded not a bit that her wedding should be put off yet again.

But that morning the duke's servant spoke to him, asking him what was the meaning of the strange singing and weeping which had been going on for the last two nights.

'I heard no singing,' said the duke. 'You must have imagined it.'

'This is no imagining,' said the man. 'This was the song of an unhappy woman. Take care not to drink too deeply tonight and stay awake, and you will learn the answer to this mystery.'

That night the duke lay as if fast asleep, and the princess came to his bedside. She wept and sighed deeply, and then she sang:

*'Far hae I sought ye,*
*Near am I brought t' ye;*
*Dear Duke o' Norroway,*
*Will ye no' turn and speak t' me?'*

He turned and opened his eyes, and knew her.

Wasn't that a meeting? They talked till dawn. The duke told her that he had been in the power of a wizard, who had used spells to bind the duke to his favourite daughter. The princess's love had broken the spell and the false bride had now fled.

Nothing stood between the duke and the princess and complete happiness. The wedding that had been three times delayed now took place, but there was another bride and far greater rejoicing. Long lived they in deep contentment, and often the princess would tease her duke by calling him 'Dear Bull'.

NORWAY

# PUSSY-GREEDYGUTS

OLD Tabbycat was employed to keep the farm free of mice, but she had such an appetite that it looked as if she would eat the farmer out of all his profits. So he hardened his heart and said that she would have to go into the river, with a stone tied around her neck to make sure.

He would not have her die with an empty belly, however, so he told his wife to give her one last good breakfast. Old Goody gave her a big bowl of porridge. Puss gobbled it down, singing quietly to herself. Then she went to see her master, waving her tail and continuing with her song.

'Good day to you, Puss,' said Master. 'Have you had a good meal?'

'I've had a small taste of porridge,' said Puss. 'But I'm still hungry. I have a fancy for a mouthful of Master.' So she swallowed him up in one gulp.

Then she went to find the farmer's wife who was in the milking-shed.

'Good day, Puss,' said the old woman. 'Have you eaten your breakfast?'

'I've had a taste,' said Puss. 'I've eaten some porridge and the master, but I'm still hungry. I guess I'll eat you.' And she gollupped down the old woman.

The cow peered down at her from her stall.

'Good day, Puss,' said Cow. 'Have you eaten well today?'

'I've had a taste,' said Puss. 'I've eaten some porridge and the master and the mistress, but I'm still hungry. I guess I'll eat you.' And down went the cow.

Puss went down the lane, and there was a hedge-cutter at his work.

'Good day, Puss,' said John Hedger. 'Have you eaten well today?'

'I've had a taste,' said Puss. 'I've eaten some porridge and the master and the mistress and the cow, but I'm still hungry. I guess I'll eat you.' And the hedge-cutter joined the others.

Puss went on down the lane until she met the fox.

'Good day, Puss,' said Fox. 'Have you eaten well to-day?'

'I've had a taste. I've eaten some porridge and the master and the mistress and the cow and the hedge-cutter, but I'm still hungry. I guess I'll eat you.' And Puss gobbled down Fox.

She wandered off into the wood and there she came up with the wolf.

'Good day, Puss,' said Wolf. 'Have you eaten well today?'

'I've had a taste. I've eaten some porridge and the master and the mistress and the cow and the hedge-cutter and the fox, but I'm still hungry. I guess I'll eat you.' And Puss swallowed up Wolf.

She wandered on and wandered on again and came to a village. A wedding was taking place, and here came the bride, dancing out of church with her man and all her friends and family.

'Good day to you on my wedding day, Puss,' said Bessie Bride. 'Have you eaten well today?'

'I've had a taste. I've eaten some porridge and the master and the mistress and the cow and the hedge-cutter and the fox and the wolf, but I'm still hungry. I guess I'll eat you.' And Puss ate up the bride and the groom and all the wedding guests.

She went along and she went along until she reached the next village. The headman had died, and everyone was following the coffin to the church.

'Good day to you this sad day, Puss,' said Michael Mourner. 'Have you eaten well today, because we have been too sad to take a bite?'

'I've had a taste. I've eaten some porridge and the master and the mistress and the cow and the hedge-cutter and the fox and the wolf and the wedding party, but I'm still hungry. I guess I'll eat you.' And Puss gobbled up the mourners and the parson and would have

eaten the coffin too, but it was too hard.

So she walked along and along and came to a bridge over a stream. On the bridge stood the billy-goat.

'Good day to you this fine day, Puss,' said Billy-goat. 'Have you eaten well today?'

'I've had a taste. I've eaten some porridge and the master and the mistress and the cow and the hedge-cutter and the fox and the wolf and the wedding party and the funeral party, but I'm still hungry. I guess I'll eat you.'

'Oh, will you?' said Billy-goat, and he put down his head and he lifted his horns and he butted that Pussy-cat just where she had put her breakfast. She shot into the air, right off the bridge and into the river, and as she reached the water she burst.

Out came the master and the mistress and the cow and the hedge-cutter and the fox and the wolf and the wedding party and the funeral party, and they all went home just as good as ever, if not better. But poor Pussy-cat was past mending.

CHINA

# A PRINCESS ON A SWING

GENERAL Chia had orders to make a journey throughout China to inspect the defences of that country, and with him he took his secretary, a young man of good family and education named Cheng, as well as the usual company of men-at-arms and servants.

One day the general's party came to a big lake. 'Here we shall make camp,' said the general. 'See to it, Cheng.'

When all was done to General Chia's satisfaction, he decided to go fishing. They sailed into the middle of the lake, and soon a very large fish was seen swimming nearby. The general took his bow and shot an arrow which hit the fish in the side. It was still alive, but so badly hurt that they had no difficulty in hauling it into the boat. It was a great ugly brute, and it had a pretty little fish hanging on to its tail. To stop it falling back into the water in its death struggles, they tied it to the mast and there it hung, gasping for breath.

To Cheng it seemed that the fish was pleading for its life. He took pity and begged the general to let it go.

General Chia roared with laughter. 'Don't say that you have fallen in love with this mermaid,' he said. 'She's too ugly for that. Still, if you want her you may have her. She doesn't look as if she would make a tasty meal, anyway.'

Cheng gladly cut the rope and let the great fish down from the mast. Then he dressed the wound in her side and had her lowered gently back into the water. The little fish was still clinging to her tail. The fish circled once around the boat, as if to show gratitude to her deliverer, and then she swam rapidly away.

Time went by. Cheng was kept busy looking after his master, as they made their way across China. Some time afterwards they returned to the great lake, and in a free hour Cheng took a small boat and went sailing. Suddenly a storm arose, and over went the boat. Cheng was thrown into deep water. He splashed about desperately and managed to get a hold on some floating wreckage. To this he clung for many hours until, as morning came, the storm died down and his refuge drifted to shore. He crawled on to dry land and lay for a time as if dead. But the warm sun revived him and, when he had dried his clothes, he set out to look for food and shelter. He was very hungry.

As he walked an arrow hummed past his ear. He threw himself down in a fright, and saw two warriors gallop past him on fine white horses. He was amazed to see that they were girls, finely dressed and very beautiful. When they were out of sight Cheng got up and, having no better plan, followed their trail up hill. He reached the top, and in the plain below he saw a whole troop of armed women, hunting a herd of deer. They looked fearsome, and rode and shot like trained soldiers, and Cheng was by no means eager to meet them. So he continued cautiously on his way. He took care to keep well away from the women, but a young man who seemed to be one of their servants saw Cheng and hastened to meet him.

'What are you doing here?' he said.

Cheng explained.

'Keep out of my mistress's way,' said the young man. 'The princess is not overfond of any man, and foreigners she hates. If she sees you, your life will not be worth a penny.'

He gave Cheng a little food from his hunting bag and sent him scurrying out of sight.

In time the track which Cheng followed led into a forest, and in the depth of this he came to a high wall, guarded by a moat. He crept across a wooden bridge and peeped through a door which stood half open.

There was the most astonishing sight: a great palace, towers and halls shining gold in the sunlight, all girt about with gardens and parkland blazing with many flowers. And most marvellous of all, instead of rising from the solid earth, the whole palace was floating gently in the air, drifting a little in a soft breeze.

Cheng was gazing at all these wonders when he heard the sound of girls' voices. A clump of tall shrubs grew on the edge of an open area of grass, and he hid among the leaves. He was no sooner out of sight than a party of the young huntswomen appeared. They flung themselves on the grass, grumbling about the poor day's hunting.

Soon another party appeared. At the centre was a young girl of the greatest loveliness. She walked across the lawn, followed by her guards, and sat down in the doorway of an open pavilion. Servants ran to pull off her hunting boots, while others brought her tea in a fine cup.

When she had drunk her fill, one of her companions untied the rope of a swing which was hanging in the open garden, seemingly suspended from the clouds. The princess sat in the swing and drifted to and fro, higher and higher until she passed right out of sight. 'Look!' said her companions. 'She is like an angel, going up into heaven.'

Cheng, who was watching from his hiding place as if two eyes were not enough to take in all this beauty, was almost aswoon with love for the beautiful princess.

Presently she tired of her play. The servants lifted her down from the swing, and they all went away into the palace.

Out came Cheng. As he walked across the grass, full of vain longings and loving thoughts, he saw something red lying on the ground. It was the princess's handkerchief, which she had dropped as she swung. He took it up and pressed it to his lips. Then—for he was a man of good education—he felt moved to write a poem. He went into the pavilion and sat down at a small table. Then taking a

brush he spread out the handkerchief and wrote on it in fine black characters:

*'Red dress and snowy feet;*
*Her beauty dims the sun.*
*Who is this angel*
*Who flies from earth*
*And then floats back from heaven?'*

While he sat there, reading his poem and devising in his head a tune to which he might sing it, a young maiden came from the palace and began searching in the grass. Not finding what she sought, she came at last to the pavilion and saw Cheng.

'What are you doing here?' she cried.

'I am only a wandering stranger,' said Cheng. 'Pray show me the way to the city, so that I may continue my travels.'

'I don't know what the princess will say,' said the young woman. 'First she loses her handkerchief, and now a strange man in her own pavilion. She will be so angry.'

'At least,' said Cheng, 'I may help in one thing. I have found the missing handkerchief, but, alas, I have dared to write upon it.'

'You are a dead man,' said the girl. 'The princess might have forgiven your intrusion, for you are clearly a man of breeding and education, but she will never pardon you for spoiling her favourite handkerchief. Wait here.'

Cheng did what he was told, although, to tell the truth, he would rather have flown into the clouds, or turned himself into an ant and hidden in a crack in the ground, to escape the princess's anger. Soon the girl came back.

'You are a fortunate young man,' she said. 'My mistress was gracious enough to read your poem. She will let you live. In time she may even set you free. Meanwhile you must swear to make no attempt to escape.'

Cheng gave his word, and indeed he had no alternative. The girl brought him food, for he had gone hungry a long time. Then she left him to his thoughts.

Hours later the girl appeared again, running with her long hair flowing wildly.

'You are lost,' she said. 'The queen has been told that you are here. She is strict against men in the palace, and has ordered your instant death.'

As she spoke, a noisy crowd came out of the palace. Cheng's hands were tied, and he was dragged to a courtyard in which the executioner waited, a dreadful black figure holding a great axe. Cheng was forced to his knees.

'Stop!' shouted someone in the crowd. It was a young girl. The executioner bowed and laid down his axe, for it was the queen's own personal attendant who had called. This girl ran off and returned quickly. 'Bring him to the queen,' she said, and Cheng was dragged, trembling in every limb, along many passages and up to a pair of stately doors.

A loud voice called out: 'The Honourable Cheng to speak with the queen.'

The doors opened. Cheng flung himself to the floor and laid his head at the queen's feet. 'Forgive an ignorant stranger, Your Majesty,' he said. 'I meant no harm to you or your kingdom.'

'You are no stranger,' said the queen. She stepped down from the throne and with her own hands she raised him. 'Bring food,' she ordered.

Cheng was in a daze. He scarcely knew what he was doing as he sat down at the queen's side while fine dishes were set before them. The queen said: 'I have read the words you wrote for my daughter. It is clear that you love her, and I should be proud for you to take her as your wife. Let the wedding take place without delay.'

It was too difficult for Cheng to find all the fine phrases and rich compliments that the occasion called for. He was only able to stammer a few words of gratitude, as the princess was brought to him and their hands joined in marriage.

Much later, when he was alone at last with his lovely bride, Cheng begged her to explain what had happened.

'Some time ago,' said the princess, 'my mother was on a journey when she was attacked from a boat. Through the kindness of a mortal she was saved from death and her wound treated. The queen owes her life to you, and I my happiness.'

'How was it that I was saved from execution?' asked Cheng.

'My mother's maid was with her on the day that she was wounded. Do you remember the little fish which clung to the big one's tail? That was the girl who recognized you just as the executioner was about to do his work.'

'How can I ever show you my gratitude?' cried Cheng.

'There is plenty of time,' said the princess. 'We are going to be married for a long time, and I will give you every chance to show whether you are satisfied with your wife.'

And indeed he never failed to make the most of these chances.

After a while Cheng began to worry about his parents who must surely believe him drowned. The queen arranged for a message to be taken to them, and later he himself returned home, travelling in great splendour and richly clad.

A strange story is told about Cheng at a later time. One of his old school friends was travelling on business. He was on a boat crossing the lake where Cheng had had his first adventures. He sailed past a richly painted houseboat from which the sound of music and merriment came. Looking down into the houseboat he saw a lovely lady lying on a couch with a handsome young man at her feet. To his surprise he recognized this man as Cheng. They talked together for a while and drank a glass of wine together, before the friend sailed on his way.

When he got home the first person he met was Cheng, who was looking very much older. 'Why, Cheng!' he said. 'How did you get home so soon? It was only yesterday that I saw you revelling on the lake.'

'Nonsense,' said Cheng. 'I have not stirred from home for the past week. You must have been drinking. Clever I may be, but I can't be in two places at once.'

The friend discussed the mystery with neighbours in the town, but no-one could come up with an explanation. But everyone agreed that there was something rather strange about Cheng.

However, there he was, living at home with his parents and growing older like any other mortal.

Then, after many years, Cheng died. He was laid in his coffin, and the funeral feast was prepared. When the moment came to carry him to the grave, the bearers who lifted the coffin cried out in amazement. 'It is so light! There can't be anything inside.' The lid was lifted, and, sure enough, the coffin was empty.

How could this be?

Listen carefully. When Cheng married his princess he became, like her, one of the immortals. But he was still a Chinese gentleman, and every Chinese owes a duty to his parents to keep them company through life and to honour them after death. The Lake Queen had, by her magic arts, granted him a double life. One part remained mortal, grew old, and died. The other stayed in the Palace of Air, immortal and eternally in love with the beautiful princess.

JAPAN

# THE DRAGON-KING'S PALACE

URASHIMA Taro was on his way home after a day's fishing when he came upon a gang of boys tormenting a turtle which they had caught. They took no notice when he appealed to them to let the creature go. But when he dipped his hand into his pocket and came out with a few coins they cheerfully gave up their victim and ran off to spend the money.

The fisher-lad then picked up the turtle, carried it to the water's edge, and let it swim away.

Next day started just like any other day. Urashima went out fishing soon after dawn.

When he was well out to sea, with no other sail in sight, he thought that he heard someone calling his name: 'Urashima Taro.' That was strange. He looked all around but there was no one to be seen. Then he noticed a turtle swimming alongside.

'Did you call, my turtle?' he asked politely.

'Yes,' said the turtle. 'I came to thank you for saving my life yesterday.'

'Come aboard,' said Urashima, and the turtle heaved itself into the boat and lay contentedly in the sun.

They stayed awhile in friendly silence; then the turtle said: 'You deserve a reward for your kindness. Have you ever seen the palace of the Dragon-King?'

'Never,' said Urashima. 'All the fishermen talk about it, but no one has ever been there.'

'Then I'll take you. Just help me over the side, and then you may ride on my back.'

The boy jumped overboard and clambered on to the turtle's hard shell. There he clung, while the creature swam on the surface for a long way. Suddenly it dived, and Urashima found himself deep in the blue water. He was taken quite by surprise and had no time to take a deep breath, but he discovered that he could breathe quite easily under the sea, and so he felt free to admire all the wonders of the deep.

A long voyage they had, but at last they came up to a great gateway, and at the turtle's word the gate was flung open and they swam into a courtyard. Before them they saw a beautiful palace all made of coral and sea-gems. Around the palace were laid four gardens, one for each season of the year, so that the king might enjoy spring blossom, summer fruits, autumn colours and ice and snow just by strolling from one garden to another.

The turtle set Urashima on his feet and told him to go wherever he wished, and the boy wandered about for a long time, marvelling at all he saw. Then, in an inner garden, he came upon a most beautiful lady, the Princess Otohime, the daughter of the Dragon-King himself. Urashima fell on his knees and set his head on the ground before her, for he had never seen anyone half as lovely and as stately.

'Stand up, Urashima,' said the princess. 'Welcome to my palace.'

'Most humble thanks, your highness.'

'No, it is for me to thank you. Know then that I was that turtle whom you saved from a cruel death. Because of your goodness I am now restored to my true self.'

Then the princess took him by the hand and led him through the gardens. Servants brought him fruit and wine, and he sat beside the princess while fish made wonderful music for them. It was not long before Urashima and the princess discovered that they were in love, and so they sought out the Dragon-King and asked his leave to marry. He made no objection, and so the marriage took place with great joy and merriment.

For a long time they were perfectly happy. Then, one morning, Urashima awoke from a dream of his home on dry land and of his mother and father. His face was wet with the tears he had shed in his longing to see them again. The princess was distressed to see his grief, and so he told her that he was homesick for a sight of his parents. They were growing old, and if he did not go soon he might never see them again.

The princess was sad to part with her husband so

quickly, but she could not stand between him and his honorable parents. 'Go, if you must, but do not forget your wife who loves you. Here, take this casket with you, and when you look at it remember me. It contains something very precious, but you must never open it. If you do, great sorrow will come upon you.'

So Urashima sadly said goodbye to his princess, and taking the casket he went to the great gate of the palace. Here a turtle took him on its back and swam with him to land.

When Urashima saw the mountains of his homeland his heart was lifted high. He waded quickly to land and looked around at the familiar scene. There was an old man standing on the shore, and just for a moment he thought that it must be his father. He ran to greet him, but when he came close he saw that it was a stranger.

So he took the path to his father's humble cottage. How strange! It was gone, and where it had once stood rose the walls of a fine big house. He knocked, and a strange man came to the door to greet him.

'Sir, do the family of Urashima Taro the fisherman live here?'

'What are you talking about?' said the man. 'Why, they have been dead these three hundred years.'

'But—I am Urashima Taro,' said the young man.

'Don't talk such nonsense,' said the man. 'They say that Urashima Taro the fisher-boy disappeared one day, long years ago. My own great-grandfather bought his house and pulled it down, and it was very old even then. Stop this joking.'

'It is no joke. I am Urashima Taro, and I am seventeen years old.'

'Urashima Taro has been gone three hundred years,' said the man. 'Go and talk to the priest. You will find the story written in the temple records.'

Urashima walked sadly away. Wherever he looked he saw that the old familiar things had gone. There was not one person that he knew, and all the houses had been rebuilt. It must be true, then. The few weeks he had spent away from home had indeed been three hundred years.

He sat weeping on the sands, looking down through the water towards the palace which he had left. How could he ever get back again?

In his arms he still carried the casket which the princess had given him. Perhaps this would help him to return. She had tied it with a golden cord. He remembered that she had warned him never to open it, but perhaps she had not realized what trouble he would find himself in.

'Forgive me, dearest wife, if I disobey you. I know not what else to do.'

He put the casket down, untied the knotted cord, and lifted the lid. It was empty. Only a breath of sweet-scented air drifted out and was lost.

He sat on the sands without moving. Then, very slowly, his youth and strength ebbed out of him. His eyes grew dim. His face fell into a thousand wrinkles, and his hair turned white as snow. His arms and legs shrank into bone, and his strong chest caved in. With a soft cry he fell forward on his face and lay still.

Next day, fishermen going down to their boats found the body of a very old man, lying on the shore with a golden casket beside him.

'Is this the fellow who spoke to you yesterday?' asked one.

'No, that was a fine, strong young man. Do you know, he tried to tell me that he was Urashima Taro! How is that for a joke?'

TURKEY

# THE MAGIC MIRROR

WHEN the old wood-cutter died, his only son decided to leave the forest where he had spent all his days and go out into the world to find a fortune. He slung his axe over his shoulder and set out.

He had walked many a mile when he heard the noise of a mighty struggle, and—see!—an elephant and a great snake locked in battle. The fight was so balanced that the result might go either way. The snake was trying to swallow the elephant whole, but one of the elephant's tusks had jammed in its throat and would not go down.

'Help me, master,' panted the elephant. 'Chop this serpent into little bits and I will be your slave for ever.'

'Take no notice of him,' said the snake. 'All I ask is one stroke of your axe. Chop off this troublesome tusk, and he will slide down smoothly, big as he is.'

It seemed to the man that this was the easier task, so he swung his axe and took off the tusk at a blow. The snake gave one gulp and the elephant slipped down into his belly with no more trouble.

'Thank you, young man,' said the snake. 'You won't regret this.' And so the two went on their way together in good fellowship.

After a while they came in sight of a big house. 'My old mother lives here,' said the snake. 'Here will we take our rest, and she will give you your reward. When I tell her what you have done she will offer you the pick of anything in the house: food or drink or jewels or money. Take none of them. Ask only for the little mirror that hangs by the door.'

The snake knocked, and his mother opened the door. 'Come in, brother,' said the snake.

'What's that?' said his mother. 'This is no brother of yours, as I should know better than anyone.'

'He who saves my life is my brother, whoever his mother may be,' said the snake, and he told her what had happened.

So the old woman welcomed them and laid food and drink for them. But the wood-cutter would not touch any of it.

'This won't do,' said the snake's mother. 'My son's deliverer must have his reward. What shall it be? A thousand pounds? The biggest diamond in the world?

You shan't go away empty-handed.'

'Very well,' said the young man. 'If you insist, I will take that little mirror that hangs by the door.'

She did not like that one little bit, but there it was. She had given her word and she could not go back on it. She took down the mirror, looked at it and shook her head sadly, and handed it to him.

Now the young man went on his way again. It seemed to him that he had not been very wise. He had refused great riches for the sake of a bit of glass. He stopped and stared into it, and then, suddenly, the glass misted and when it cleared again an enormous genie stood before him.

'What is your command, master?' said this being.

'Well, knock me down with a feather!' stammered the young man in surprise, and that is what the genie did.

He staggered to his feet and rubbed his head. Then he said to the genie: 'I'd like a good feed.'

The genie vanished, and where he had stood there was a fine banquet laid out, the like of which the young man had not seen in all his life.

It did not seem right that all this fine food should lie there in the forest, so he said: 'I want a palace.'

The trees faded, and he found himself standing in the courtyard of a great palace, all built of marble and gold and ivory. Before him stood the banqueting hall, and the feast was spread out ready for eating. Only one thing was lacking, so the wood-cutter summoned the genie again and asked for a princess. In the twitch of an eyelid there she was, the loveliest princess in the world, and pleased to see him too. They kissed, and sat down to their feast together.

The young man was delighted with his good fortune. The trouble was that the princess was a real princess, not a magical one, and she had a real father too. He was the king, and he was very angry when his only daughter disappeared. He offered big rewards to anyone who could bring her back.

An old woman offered to earn the reward. She ordered a big box to be made, well lined with zinc, and with food enough for a week. When all was ready, she climbed inside, and the box was carried to the shore and thrown into the sea.

For a whole week the box drifted on the waves, tossed this way and that by the currents, and on the last day it came to rest on the beach, close by the palace where our wood-cutter was enjoying life with his princess.

Some fishermen dragged the box to dry land. They forced off the lid, and out crawled the old woman. 'However did you get in there?' they asked.

'Oh, what a wicked man it is!' she cried. 'I never deserved to be treated like this,' and she shouted and screamed as if she had lost her senses.

'Who is the ruler here?' she said. 'Surely he will give me justice.'

So they took her to the palace, and she knocked on the door. The wood-cutter was away from home, and the princess opened to her.

'I am a poor ill-used woman,' she said. 'Please give me shelter, and I will work hard for you.'

The princess took pity on her and let her stay. The old woman soon found that this was no ordinary palace. No servants were to be seen, no kitchen or sign of cooking, yet everything was clean and tidy and the finest food appeared on the table at each meal.

She said to the princess one day: 'This is a wonderful house, Highness. How comes it that we feed so well and that all the house is a miracle of cleanliness, and yet no servant is to be seen?'

'I cannot say,' said the princess. 'All that is my husband's concern, and he has told me nothing.'

'Ask him how it is done,' said the old woman.

When the wood-cutter returned home, the princess was more loving than ever and they were happy together. But she had become curious, and could not wait to ask him where his fortune came from. At first he was unwilling to talk about it, but she pressed him hard and at last he gave way and told her the secret of the mirror. She in turn lost no time in telling the old woman.

'What a wonderful toy! Wouldn't you like to play with it yourself?' the old woman said cunningly. 'Why not ask him to lend it to you?'

This the princess did, and he could refuse her nothing. The princess hid the precious mirror in a safe place, but the old woman spied on her. When the princess became busy in another part of the palace, she took out the mirror, looked into it, and at once the genie appeared.

'What is your command, mistress?'

'Take me and the princess back to her father's palace.'

It was done in a moment. Then the old woman summoned the genie again, and ordered him to destroy the wood-cutter's palace by fire.

When he came home from the day's hunting, the

wood-cutter found that at one stroke he had lost both wife and home. Nothing was left but a heap of ashes, and the cat poking among them, mewing and hunting for food. The wood-cutter looked too, and there among the ashes lay a plain gold ring which he knew was one he had given the princess.

He picked up the ring and went in search of his wife. Far and wide he wandered through many countries until he came to the city where the princess's father ruled. He went to the palace and begged for work, and the cook took pity on him and let him do the unskilled work of the kitchen.

One day the cook was taken ill and could not prepare the meal for the royal household, so the wood-cutter took his place and made a rich and tempting dish. He sent up the food to the dining room, and on the princess's plate he hid the ring. The princess recognized it at once and she ordered that the cook who had made this meal should bring coffee to her room. So he came and they were together again.

After their first kisses, she told her husband all that had happened and that the old woman, who now stood high in the king's favour, still had the mirror. They discussed for a long time how they might get it back. But while they still talked, the old woman came into the room and recognized him at once. Back she ran to her room, called up the genie, and ordered him to take the wood-cutter and drop him among the ashes of his palace.

In a flash it was done. The cat was waiting for him among the ruins. This good creature at once set about catching food for her poor master. For herself she killed nothing but mice, and so skilled a hunter did she become that soon the kingdom of mice was in a desperate state. The mouse king knew not what to do to save his people from this whiskered terror. At last he came to the woodcutter and pleaded for his help.

'I will use what influence I have,' said the young man. 'And indeed my good puss will surely not want to destroy her own food supply utterly. Alas, I wish there were as easy an answer to my own problem.'

'What problem is that?' said the mouse king. So the young man told him the whole story.

'I think I may be able to do something about that,' said the mouse king, and he called his people together and told them what the problem was.

'I know that old woman,' said an old lame mouse. 'I have often been in the palace and stolen food from her box. She has a little mirror which she hides under the cushions of her couch.'

'Get me that mirror,' ordered the mouse king.

'Give me two companions,' said the lame mouse. 'Or I shall be all day getting there on these twisted legs of mine.' So off he went with two strong young mice, riding on one and with the other running alongside.

When they got there, the old woman was just finishing her supper. They crept in and stole the crumbs as they fell to the floor. Then they hid until she had settled down to sleep.

The old mouse climbed up on to the pillow and tickled the old woman's nose with his long tail. She stirred, grunted and then sneezed—'Tschoo!'—so hard that her head nearly came away from her body. She rolled over, gasping for breath, and up jumped the two young mice and snatched the mirror. The old mouse scrambled on to

his companion's back and they were away.

The wood-cutter rejoiced to see them. He took the mirror, whistled for his cat, and set off with her until they reached a quiet spot. Then he summoned the genie.

'What is your command, master?'

'Armour, and a troop of soldiers, and a good horse.'

At once they were there. He put on his armour, mounted his steed, and led the troops to the palace where his princess was waiting. The king, her father, took one look at the fierce soldiers and surrendered. He gave up his daughter and his kingdom too, so that the wood-cutter became a king and a good one he made, too.

There was still the problem of what to do with the old woman. The new king and his wife talked about this long into the night. Then he took the mirror and looked into it. There stood the enormous genie.

'What is your command, master?'

'Take this troublesome old woman, marry her, and see that she does no more mischief.'

So it was done, and the king and queen lived together in happiness all their days. They kept the mirror close at hand to supply their every need.

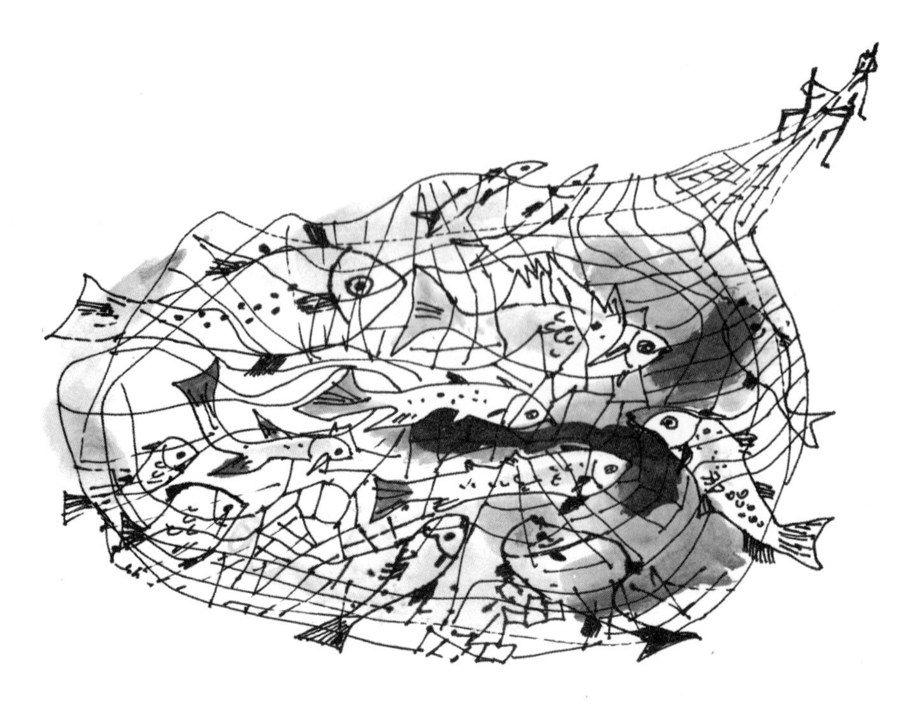

NEW ZEALAND

# HUIA'S DREAM

HUIA the mighty chief dreamed a dream. Three nights running it came to him in the darkest hour. It seemed to him that he saw his tribe, not poor, scraping a hard living from a reluctant earth, but rich and happy. And a voice spoke to him in the silence of his brain, saying: 'Go forth, alone. Seek out a land in the farthest north. There you will find what you seek, a treasure that will enrich your people.'

For a time he kept this dream to himself. Then he discussed it with the elders of the tribe. They would not agree that he might travel alone, for the chief must have always his bodyguard with him. To this Huia said nothing. He had no wish to break the laws of the people, but the voice in his dream had spoken clearly: he must go alone.

So one day, at dawn, after a night of feasting which left all the tribe lying in deep sleep, Huia arose and took his spear and went alone on the northward trail.

He travelled for many days, walking through all the long hours of daylight and often into the night, too, because a clear northern star seemed to lead him on. He grew very weary, and disheartened too, for the first excitement of his vision had faded and the long rocky coast seemed to go on for ever. But at last a day came when the shoreline began to curve towards the east. He had reached his farthest north.

Huia looked about him. There was nothing to mark this from other places, and the voice of his vision remained silent.

He felt very tired. Looking for a place to rest, he found a bush and lay down, quite hidden by the tall leaves. There he slept.

He was awakened by sounds of music. It was night and a full moon shone. He stood up and peeped through the leaves. The sea was covered with canoes, filled with very small men and women, all singing as they swung to their paddles. They came to the sands and hauled up their craft; then they formed up in groups and began to dance.

Never had Huia seen such dancing. The little people seemed light as air as they leapt and tossed their fair hair.

Some of the folk broke away from the dance and ran

into the shallow water, pulling something between them. As they came to land, Huia saw that they were holding a light, finely woven fabric, and that it was full of tossing fish. The little people ran to the fishermen, gathered up their catch and prepared for a feast.

Was this the meaning of my dream? thought Huia. He had never seen fish caught in such a way before. His own people used to wade into the waves, trying to catch fish with a spear. It was slow and dangerous work, and only the most skilled men ever made a catch. This strange catcher of fish must surely be the treasure he had come so far to find.

The little people finished eating and turned to play, running and chasing in the moonlight. One maiden, fairer and slimmer than any of the others, ran past Huia's hiding-place with a young man in close pursuit. Her laughter sounded like the rarest kind of music. Using the shadow of the bush to escape, she threw herself among the leaves and lay still, while the man blundered on and lost her. Huia kept silent and watched her unseen.

Now, when Huia's tribe awoke after their feast and found that their chief had left them, they were greatly troubled. They called out two men who were skilled in tracking, and sent them on Huia's trail. Now, when the frolic of the little people was at its height, these two men appeared. At once the dancers were thrown into panic. They ran in all directions. Two of them picked up the fishing fabric, but managed to get it entangled in the bush where Huia and the maiden were hidden, and so they abandoned it there. Now all ran to the canoes. The maiden jumped up and would have followed her companions, but she tripped and was caught like a fish. Try as she would she could not escape the clinging folds.

'Help me!' she cried. 'I am caught in the net.'

'The net!' said Huia. 'So that is what it is called. I will take this net to my people and it will make them great. And I will take the catch too.' And he strode over and took the struggling maiden in his arms.

'Be not afraid,' he said. 'The net will be my people's blessing, and you will be mine.'

She looked up at the chief. Love entered her heart and she ceased struggling.

The little people paddled away out of sight, and Huia returned to his people, taking his bride with him.

She taught the tribe how to make nets, and with these they prospered and became great, just as Huia's dream had foretold. But Huia hung the first net in the roof of his house, as a reminder that his wife had been his first and most precious catch.

GERMANY

## THE FISHERMAN'S WIFE

THERE was this fisherman. He lived with his wife in an old pigsty by the sea. He went fishing every day. As for his wife, she stayed at home and tried to clean the house, and there was little she could do about that.

One fine day the fisherman went fishing, and there he sat, and there he sat. Then—see!—there goes his float, down, down, in the clear water. He pulled it up, and he had a big fish on his hook.

'Look you here, fisherman,' said the fish. 'Put me back. I'm not really a fish. I'm a prince under enchantment. Put me back, there's a good fellow. Besides, I'd taste something horrid.'

'No need to waste all those words,' said the fisherman. 'A talking fish, eh? I wouldn't keep one of them anyway.'

So he dropped the fish back, and down it dived, leaving a little thread of blood behind it in the water.

The fisherman got up and went home.

'What's this?' said the wife. 'You've caught nothing again?'

'Well,' said the man. 'I did catch a fish, but he said he was an enchanted prince, so I let him go.'

'Didn't you ask for something first?'

'No. What could I ask for?'

'What?' said the woman. 'Here we are, stuck in a filthy old pigsty, and you can't think of anything to ask for! Go back to the fish and ask for a little hut. He won't say no to that, that's for sure.'

'Nay,' said the man. 'I don't want to ask the fish for anything.'

'Be off with you,' said the wife, and as he always did what she told him he went, but he didn't like it.

He came to the sea, and it was no longer calm and clear but ruffled and smeared with green and yellow. He stood and said:

*'Enje menje tyne 'n tee!*
*Fishie fishie, come to me.*
*Ilsebil my wayward wife*
*Wants to change our way of life.'*

'What does she want, then?' said the fish.

'Fair's fair,' said the man. I did let you go, didn't I? She's tired of our pigsty. What she wants is a little hut.'

'Go home,' said the fish. 'She has it.'

So the fisherman went home, and there stood a neat little hut with his wife sitting outside.

'There!' said the wife. 'Isn't that better? Come and see.'

She led him inside, and it was all clean and smart, with a bed and a cooking stove and all they could want. At the back there was a garden with a goat and hens and some fruit trees.

'That's more like, isn't it?' said the wife.

'Surely,' said the man. 'We can rest content now.'

'Let us see about that,' said his wife. So they had some food and went to bed.

It went on like that for a week or two. Then the woman said: 'Look here, man. There's no room to move in this hut. We keep bumping into one another. The fish could do better than that. Go and tell him I want a castle.'

'No,' said the man. 'That is not right. The hut is good enough. We don't want a castle.'

'I want a castle,' she said. 'Go and tell him.'

'He won't like it,' said the man. 'I don't want to make him angry.'

'Go!' said the wife. 'He will do this for us.'

He wasn't happy, but still he went. The sea was dark now, purple and grey, but it was still quiet. He stood and said:

*'Enje menje tyne 'n tee!*
*Fishie fishie, come to me.*

*Ilsebil my wayward wife*
*Wants to change our way of life.'*

'What does she want, then?' said the fish.

'She wants a castle,' said the man.

'Go home. She has it.'

So he went home and, instead of the hut, there stood a fine stone castle. Steps led up to the gate, and at the foot stood the wife.

'Come and see,' she said, and led him by the hand. Inside, it was all stone and marble. Servants opened doors for them, and every room was hung with cloth-of-gold. Tables and chairs were of gold too, and the side-boards groaned under heaps of food, all of the best. Outside there was a big garden and a park with deer.

'There, isn't that good?' said the wife.

'Surely,' said the man. 'We can be well content with all this.'

'That we shall see.' So they ate a big meal and went to bed.

They slept late, and when the wife awoke she looked out of the window and saw all the land bathed in sun-shine. She dug her husband in the ribs with her elbow, and said: 'Get up, man. See all that land. You could be king over all of it. Go and ask the fish.'

'What's that?' said the man. 'King? I don't want to be king.'

'If you don't want to be king, I do,' said the wife. 'Go to the fish at once.'

The man got up, muttering: 'Why should you want to be king? It's not right.' But he went, all the same, and all the way he kept saying to himself: 'It is not right.'

The sea was a dirty grey and the water churned from deep down, and it had a bad stink to it. He stood and said:

> *'Enje menje tyne 'n tee!*
> *Fishie fishie, come to me.*
> *Ilsebil my wayward wife*
> *Wants to change our way of life.'*

'What does she want, then?' said the fish.

'What does she want?' said the man. 'She wants to be king.'

'Go home,' said the fish. 'That's what she is.'

So he went, and the castle had grown ten times bigger. There were tall towers with soldiers on them, and they blew their trumpets and fired guns. There was no sign of his wife, so he went in through gates of solid gold, and up stairs set with precious stones. In the great hall he found his wife sitting on a throne of gold. She had a crown on her head and a sceptre in her hand, and at her side stood beautiful maidens, each one a head shorter than her neighbour.

He stood and looked and said: 'So you are king, wife.'

'Yes. I am king.'

'That is good,' said the man. 'Let us leave it at that. King you are and king you shall be.'

'No,' said the wife. 'It won't do. I haven't enough to keep me busy. Go to the fish. King I am; Emperor I shall be.'

'You can't be Emperor,' said the man. 'That can't be. The fish cannot and cannot do it.'

'Go,' said the wife. 'I will be Emperor.'

So he went, and he said to himself: 'It won't do. The fish will not be pleased. Emperor is wrong. The fish will get tired.' But he went to the sea. It was black all over, and the water was thick like treacle, and bubbles boiled up from the depths. The wind howled. The man stood and said:

*'Enje menje tyne 'n tee!*
*Fishie fishie, come to me.*
*Ilsebil my wayward wife*
*Wants to change our way of life'.*

'What does she want, then?' said the fish.

'She wants to be Emperor.'

'Go home,' said the fish. 'She is that.'

He went home, and the great castle had vanished. In its place there stood a huge marble palace. An army was marching around the walls playing loud music. Inside, the place was full of lords and dukes, all working like servants. He went into the hall, and there sat his wife. She was on a throne which stood about two miles high and was made of pure gold. Her crown was so tall that it touched the roof, and he had to shade his eyes from the dazzle of the diamonds and other jewels which she wore. She was guarded by two rows of soldiers, each smaller than his neighbour, from a giant two miles high to a dwarf the size of your little finger. Princes and royal dukes bowed before her.

The fisherman stood and looked up at her and said: 'Now you are Emperor.'

'Yes,' she said. 'We are Emperor.'

He said: 'That is good. Now you can want nothing more.'

She fidgetted on her throne. Then she screamed at him: 'Don't just stand there. Go to the fish. I want to be Pope.'

'Wife!' he said. 'You can't be Pope. King and Emperor come easily to the fish, but there is only one Pope. Be satisfied.'

'Man!' she said. 'I will be Pope and I will be. I won't wait another hour. Go to the fish.'

'Do not and do not ask that,' said the man. 'I can't ask that of the fish. It is too much. We shall lose all.'

'Go to the fish,' she said. 'I am Emperor and you are my husband. Obey!'

So he went. He felt sick with fear, and he could scarcely walk for the trembling in his legs. It was getting

dark and a gale of wind had got up. The sea was boiling with rage, and he could see many ships in trouble out in the deep. The sky was a smoky red with just one small patch of blue.

So he went and stood and said:

*'Enje menje tyne 'n tee!*
*Fishie fishie, come to me.*
*Ilsebil my wayward wife*
*Wants to change our way of life.'*

'What does she want?' said the fish.

'She wants to be Pope.'

'Go home,' said the fish. 'She is.'

He went home. The palace had gone. There stood a great church, and all around it were splendid palaces. There were crowds of people everywhere, all on their knees. He fought his way through them and went into the church. It was dark, apart from the flames from many thousands of candles. He made his way to the head of the building where a golden throne rose three miles into the roof. Sitting on this he saw his wife, dressed in golden robes. She wore three crowns, one on top of another. On the steps of the throne stood candles, the biggest three miles high, the smallest a little wafer, and on each step knelt a king or an emperor, awaiting his turn to climb to the top and kiss the Pope's shoe.

The fisherman stood and looked. Then he said: 'Wife, you are now Pope.'

'We are Pope,' she said.

'That is very good,' he said. 'Pope is good. Now you can want nothing.'

'We shall think about that,' she said, and they went to bed. The man was tired out, because he had spent the day in running to the beach, but his wife could not get to sleep. She tossed and turned, wondering always what she might ask for next, and she could think of nothing better than Pope.

The night passed slowly, but at last the light in their room began to grow. She sat up in bed and looked out of the window. She saw the sun edging its way over the horizon. At once she screamed aloud and dug her husband hard in the ribs with her elbow.

'Man!' she shouted. 'Get up and go to the fish. I want to make the sun rise and set. I want to be like God.'

The man was barely awake, but in his fright he fell

right out of bed. He looked up at his wife and said: 'What is that you said?'

'Go to the fish,' she said. 'Do you think that I can lie here and watch the sun rise every morning and do nothing about it? I shall have no rest until I am master of the sun. I must be like God.'

He threw himself on his knees. 'Don't make me,' he said. 'Pope is good. The fish was willing. But this he will not and he cannot do. Have pity!'

She looked at him and her face was terrible to see. Then she tore her hair and her nightgown and screamed. She kicked him and shouted: 'Go to the fish. I can't bear it another minute.'

So he ran, half-dressed as he was, and came to the sea. The wind blew so that he could not stand upright. Trees lay where they had fallen, torn from their roots, and the earth itself tossed and twisted. The sky was jet black and the sea rose in mountains of dark waves, their tops torn to shreds of white foam.

He stood among the tumult and shouted:

*'Enje menje tyne 'n tee!*
*Fishie fishie, come to me.*
*Ilsebil my wayward wife*
*Wants to change our way of life.'*

'What does she want?' said the fish.

'She wants to make the sun rise. She wants to be like God.'

'Go home,' said the fish. 'She is back in the pigsty.'

And there you will find them living to this day.

## NOT FOR THE CHILDREN: A NOTE FOR ADULTS

My main objective in making this collection is to bring pleasure to children, and to their parents too, by telling some very good tales. The origins of all the basic themes of literature are to be found in oral folk-tales, and I have tried to illustrate the range and variety of these stories; tragedy, fantasy, romance, and broad comedy, together with many other moods, are represented here.

While my first concern has been for quality I have on the whole looked for stories which, in the form here presented, are unfamiliar, although I must confess that I was unable to omit one or two personal favourites which are known to everyone. Notable among these is the final tale which, in the version written down by the Brothers Grimm, is one of the most familiar, as it is one of the best, of all folk-tales. It is unusual among peasant-tales in its perfection of form; the unsophisticated and illiterate genius who shaped it had a rare sense of pace and mastery in the selection of significant detail.

Most of the stories are far less familiar, yet nearly all will strike a chord in adult readers. We have been here before, but the detail, or the atmosphere, or the sequence of events is different. One of the world's unsolved mysteries—although folk-lorists have their theories—is the emergence of the same tale in places widely disparate in geography or culture. So, in my collection, we find 'Cinderella' in Korea, 'Puss-in-Boots' in Hungary, 'Cat and Mouse Keep House' among the slaves of America, 'The Brave Little Tailor' in Greece. Such parallels are very close, but in every tale there is some detail—episode, character or concept—to which some likeness can be found in the familiar collections of Grimm or Asbjornsen. It matters little whether this came about through the activities of itinerant story-tellers or whether native story-tellers drew upon a common stock of human experience; what is important is that we and our children should have access to a basic literature through which we have communion with our earliest ancestors.

Most of the principal collections of folk-tales were made between 150 and a hundred years ago, many of them by anthropologists and etymologists who were concerned with them primarily not as entertainment but as material evidence for use in their sciences. Whether set down exactly as received or turned into 'literature' they rarely speak in a living language to modern children. In my new versions I have tried to get back to the oral tradition and set the tales down in modern colloquial words, through which their message can come across the centuries in all its vitality and humour. If my phrases come easily to the tongue of today's story-tellers, or if they raise a chuckle or awake a sense of wonder in the drowsy child as bed-time tales, my efforts will have been rewarded.

*Marcus Crouch*